12-7
14-5
15-F
15-6
15-11

HAMMER TIME

Out of the corner of his eye, Fargo glimpsed movement and instinctively sidestepped as Koons slashed at his leg. The knife missed by a mere whisker's width.

Fury gripped Fargo. Sheer, pounding fury. He had tried to go easy on the lunkhead, but now his Colt leaped into his hand and he brought the barrel smashing down once, twice, three times. After the third blow, Koons's nose and cheek were blood-spattered pulp. Uttering a low groan, Harve Koons pitched onto his face, twitched a bit, and was still.

None of the onlookers or passersby was disposed to come to his aid. In fact, one man commented, "About time that jackass got what he deserved."

THE TRAILSMAN

#315

MISSOURI MANHUNT

by

Jon Sharpe

A SIGNET BOOK

SIGNET
Published by New American Library, a division of
Penguin Group (USA) Inc., 375 Hudson Street,
New York, New York 10014, USA
Penguin Group (Canada), 90 Eglinton Avenue East, Suite 700, Toronto,
Ontario M4P 2Y3, Canada (a division of Pearson Penguin Canada Inc.)
Penguin Books Ltd., 80 Strand, London WC2R 0RL, England
Penguin Ireland, 25 St. Stephen's Green, Dublin 2,
Ireland (a division of Penguin Books Ltd.)
Penguin Group (Australia), 250 Camberwell Road, Camberwell, Victoria 3124,
Australia (a division of Pearson Australia Group Pty. Ltd.)
Penguin Books India Pvt. Ltd., 11 Community Centre, Panchsheel Park,
New Delhi - 110 017, India
Penguin Group (NZ), 67 Apollo Drive, Rosedale, North Shore 0632,
New Zealand (a division of Pearson New Zealand Ltd.)
Penguin Books (South Africa) (Pty.) Ltd., 24 Sturdee Avenue,
Rosebank, Johannesburg 2196, South Africa

Penguin Books Ltd., Registered Offices:
80 Strand, London WC2R 0RL, England

First published by Signet, an imprint of New American Library,
a division of Penguin Group (USA) Inc.

First Printing, January 2008
10 9 8 7 6 5 4 3 2 1

The first chapter of this book previously appeared in *North Country Cutthroats*,
the three hundred fourteenth volume in this series.

Copyright © Penguin Group (USA) Inc., 2008
All rights reserved

 REGISTERED TRADEMARK—MARCA REGISTRADA

Printed in the United States of America

PUBLISHER'S NOTE
This is a work of fiction. Names, characters, places, and incidents either are the
product of the author's imagination or are used fictitiously, and any resemblance to
actual persons, living or dead, events, or locales is entirely coincidental.
    The publisher does not have any control over and does not assume any respon-
sibility for author or third-party Web sites or their content.

The Trailsman

Beginnings . . . they bend the tree and they mark the man. Skye Fargo was born when he was eighteen. Terror was his midwife, vengeance his first cry. Killing spawned Skye Fargo, ruthless, cold-blooded murder. Out of the acrid smoke of gunpowder still hanging in the air, he rose, cried out a promise never forgotten.

The Trailsman they began to call him all across the West: searcher, scout, hunter, the man who could see where others only looked, his skills for hire but not his soul, the man who lived each day to the fullest, yet trailed each tomorrow. Skye Fargo, the Trailsman, the seeker who could take the wildness of a land and the wanting of a woman and make them his own.

The lush, green state of Missouri, 1861—
where the deep woods hid the dark heart of evil,
and death awaited the unwary.

1

If there was anything worse than a drunk spoiling for a fight, it was a drunk with a knife spoiling for a fight.

Skye Fargo coldly regarded the angry man in front of him. Fargo had been about to enter Bassiter's, a popular saloon along the public square in Springfield, Missouri. He had stepped to the batwings just as the drunk did the same on the other side. Neither had been watching what he was doing. Fargo was admiring a lovely lady who happened to be strolling by. The drunk was staring at his own feet. Fargo pushed on the batwings a split second before the drunk, with the result that the batwings caught the man flush in the face. With a startled grunt, the man had whipped his knife from a belt sheath on his hip, and now here they stood, Fargo with one hand on an open batwing, the man glaring and swaying and reeking of liquor.

"You damn near busted my nose, you son of a bitch!"

Fargo did not want trouble. He was on his way west and had stopped in Springfield for the night to treat himself to whiskey, women and cards. But neither did he like being insulted. "Not on purpose."

"I don't care," the drunk belligerently snarled. "I have half a mind to cut you." The man was almost as tall as Fargo but not as broad at the shoulders. He had droopy jowls and a paunch. His clothes, which were in need of a washing and mending, and his scuffed shoes with holes in them, marked him as a townsman, someone who, if he held a job, spent most of his money on his pet vice.

"You are drunk, mister," Fargo told him. "Put that pigsticker away before someone gets hurt."

"I already am hurt," the man declared, slurring his words. "Now it is your turn."

It was pushing nine o'clock and the street was alive with people enjoying Springfield's nightlife. A few stopped to watch, idly curious as to the outcome. One was the lovely young woman Fargo had been admiring. She was a brunette with as shapely a figure as a man could ask for, and full red lips that reminded Fargo of ripe cherries. She had lively brown eyes and full cheeks, and when she spoke, a throaty purr of a voice that would make any man tingle.

"Harve Koons, you let this gentleman be, you hear?"

The drunk squinted at her. Her beauty apparently made no impression. "Mind your own business, Lucille Sparks. I don't tell you what to do and you will not tell me."

"I saw the whole thing," the young woman responded. "It was an accident, plain and simple."

"He hurt me and I don't like being hurt." Harve Koons wagged his knife at Fargo. "Back up, mister, and do it real slow. The cutting is about to commence."

"I will go for the law," Lucille Sparks said.

"Do whatever you want, girl. It won't change anything. I will have this bastard's nose for a keepsake."

Fargo kept his eyes on the knife. He had a knife of his own, in an ankle sheath, and a Colt strapped to his waist, but he did not want to resort to either if he could help it. "I don't want any trouble," he said. Particularly with the law.

"Isn't that a shame," Koons mocked him, "because you have trouble, and plenty. Ask anyone. Ask Lucy there. I am not a man to be trifled with."

Fargo simmered with rising anger. What he had here was a local tough who felt the need to prove how tough he was. "For the last time I am asking you, polite like, to put that knife back in its sheath. I will even buy you a drink to show you there are no hard feelings on my part."

2

"There are hard feelings on mine, plainsman."

Koons's comment referred to the fact that Fargo was dressed in buckskins, the trademark of a frontiersman. Fargo also wore a white hat, brown with trail dust, and boots equally as dusty. A red bandanna added a splash of color.

"If you know what I am," Fargo said, "you know I won't stand for being pushed around." Frontiersmen were a hardy breed. They had to be. Living on the raw edge day in and day out tended to weed out the weak. It honed those who survived to a razor's edge of steely sinews and sharp reflexes.

"You long-haired types are all the same," Koons snapped. "You strut around like you own the world."

"My hair is not all that long," Fargo noted. Neither was his beard.

"Enough jawing!" Koons wagged his knife. "Back up, I say, or I will gut you where you stand!"

Lucille Sparks made a sniffing sound. "You are despicable, Harve Koons. I want you to know that."

"I thought you were going for a tin star, Lucy." Koons countered, then snickered. "Or could it be you have a hankering to share a drink with me after I am through with this peckerwood?"

"I would rather eat dirt."

Koons laughed, and glanced at her, and the instant his bloodshot eyes were off Fargo, Fargo struck. A lightning lunge, and Fargo had Koons by the wrist. With a powerful wrench, Fargo jerked him through the batwings. Koons bleated in surprise and swung his fist, but Fargo easily blocked it and drove his knee up and in.

Gurgling and wheezing, Harve Koons fell to his knees. Spittle dribbled over his lower lip as he clutched himself and turned the same shade as a turnip.

Now it was Lucille Sparks who snickered. "Oh, my. But if ever a simpleton deserved it, he did."

That was when Fargo made his mistake. He assumed Koons was in too much pain to do anything, and he started to turn toward her to thank her for trying to help. Out of the corner of his eye, he glimpsed movement and

3

instinctively sidestepped just as Koons slashed at his leg. The knife missed by a mere whisker's width.

Fury gripped Fargo. Sheer, pounding fury. He had tried to go easy on the lunkhead, but now his Colt leaped into his hand and he brought the barrel smashing down once, twice, three times. After the third blow, Koons's nose and cheek were blood-spattered pulp. Uttering a low groan, Harve Koons pitched onto his face, twitched a bit, and was still.

None of the onlookers or passersby was disposed to come to his aid. In fact, one man commented, "About time that jackass got what he deserved."

Fargo bent and wiped the Colt clean on Koons's shirt. As he was sliding it into his holster, he noticed the young lovely staring at him, appraising him much as a horse buyer might appraise a fine stallion. "It is too bad you had to see that, ma'am."

"I have seen a lot worse," Lucille Sparks said, and smiled. "Well, I should be going."

Fargo caught up with her before she had taken three steps. "What is your hurry? I was thinking I would like to treat you to coffee." He almost said whiskey but she did not strike him as a frequenter of saloons.

"You are a stranger, sir," Lucille said, not unkindly, "and ladies are taught to be wary of strangers. Especially handsome ones."

Fargo chuckled, and doffed his hat. "How about polite ones? I promise to behave myself. If I don't, you have my permission to slap me."

"I would slap you anyway," Lucille said, and lightly laughed. "All right. I suppose it can't hurt. And it is early yet. How about up ahead there? The Kettle and Drumstick?"

The Kettle and Drumstick it was. Suppertime was over and only a few of the tables were occupied. Fargo picked a corner table as much for the quiet and privacy as for the fact that he could sit with his back to the wall and watch the comings and goings. He remembered to pull out Lucille's chair for her, and for a brief moment after she sat he placed his hand on her shoulder. She did not object or swat his hand away. Taking his seat, he said, "I should thank Harve Koons. If not for him, we would not have met."

"I can't quite believe I am sitting here with you," Lucille said. "This is most bold of me."

"More kind than bold," Fargo said, hoping she would not change her mind. He liked how her bosom swelled against her dress, and imagined what it would be like to taste those cherry-red lips.

"As for Mr. Koons," Lucille went on, "he is an example of why Springfield has a lot of growing to do before it is safe for a woman to walk down the street without being accosted."

"Koons has tried to force himself on you?" Fargo would not put it past the man if he were drunk enough.

"He has made a few improper remarks but that is the extent of it," Lucille answered. "He knows my employer, Mr. Huddleston at the feed and grain, would not stand for anything worse." She paused. "I suppose I should have stayed in Ohio."

"That is where you are from?"

Lucille nodded. "Born and raised. My father runs a mercantile in Dayton. I could be working there and earn twice what I earn here. And there are not nearly as many incidents as the one you just had."

"Let me guess. You wanted some excitement in your life so you came west."

"Not exactly. I came here on a personal matter and decided to stay awhile. Life here is not anything like I thought it would be. I much prefer safe and quiet to raw and wild."

The Mississippi River, as Fargo well knew, was the boundary line between civilization and savagery. East of the great river the laws and rules of civilized society applied. West of it, except for a few widely scattered towns and settlements, hostiles and renegade whites roamed at will and slew with bloodthirsty abandon. Missouri, specifically southwest Missouri, was a mix of both worlds. There was law, and law officers to enforce it, but there were also a lot of lawbreakers, cutthroats and outlaws who struck at random and then fled into the wild haunts lawmen rarely penetrated.

Fargo was about to make more small talk, to ask her about her family in Ohio, about her job, anything to keep her there, when the door suddenly slammed open and in stormed the last person he wanted to see again.

Harve Koons had given up the knife in favor of a double-barreled shotgun. He spotted them right away, and with the stock wedged to his shoulder, advanced on their corner table with as grim an expression as the Angel of Death. "I've got you!" he crowed. "I've got you now, bastard!"

Fargo made no attempt to stand or to go for his Colt. Not with that cannon trained on him. A blast would blow him near in half.

Lucille, though, swiveled in her chair. "What do you think you are doing, Harve?"

"What does it look like?" Koons rejoined. "I asked everyone on the street where you two had gotten to and found someone who saw you come in here. Now I aim to pay your friend back for what he did to me."

"You brought it on yourself," Lucille said. "Take that silly shotgun and go sober up. You are making a spectacle of yourself."

Fargo wished she would not rile Koons more than he already was. A twitch of Koons's finger and the two of them would be splattered on the walls. As drunk as Koons was, that could happen at any moment. Ever so slowly, Fargo lowered his right hand under the table.

"I mean it," Lucille declared when Koons did not leave. "I will report you if you do not desist."

"If you know what is good for you, you will shut your mouth and get out of the way." Koons sighted down the twin barrels at Fargo. "I don't have a clear shot."

"And you won't because I am not leaving," Lucille informed him. "If you shoot him, you must shoot me, and you know what they do to men who kill women in these parts, don't you?"

Koons scowled, as well he might. Women were at a

premium in the border country. Harming one was a sure-fire invite to a strangulation jig at the end of a rope.

"Damn you, you contrary female."

"I will thank you not to talk to me in that manner," Lucille said. "I am not one of your dance hall trollops."

Fargo's hand found the butt of his Colt. He slowly drew it and leveled it under the table. But now he had the same problem Koons did. He did not have a clear shot with Lucille sitting there.

Koons seemed to have forgotten him. "You sure do put on airs, lady. You are no better than they are, no better at all."

"I do not lift my skirt for any man who buys me a drink," Lucille said tartly.

"It might be better for you if you did," Koons responded. "It would get you off your high horse and take some of the starch out of those petticoats of yours."

Lucille flushed. "When I said you were despicable earlier, I had no idea *how* despicable."

"Insult me all you want. I have a real thick hide." Koons gestured with the shotgun. "Now get the hell out of my way or I swear to God you will be pushing up daisies, female or not."

Fargo hoped she would heed, but to his considerable amazement she stood up and moved so the twin muzzles were inches from her bosom.

"Go ahead," Lucille said, defiantly glaring at Koons. "Prove how brave a man you are. I dare you."

Koons was equally amazed. "You crazy cow! Are you trying to get yourself blown to eternity?"

"I am calling your bluff," Lucille said. "Either shoot an unarmed woman or slink back to whatever hovel you live in with your tail between your legs."

Harve Koons opened his mouth but did not appear to quite know what to say. He glanced at the waitress and the other diners, who were frozen with fear, and then at Lucille. "Damn it. You are making a fool out of me."

Lucille's smile dripped sarcasm. "You give me too much credit. You do that quite well without any help from me or anyone else."

"Enough!" Koons barked. "I have put up with all I am going to. Stay out of my way or take buckshot. It is up to you." So saying, he took a step to the right so he had a clear shot at Fargo. "Any last words, mister, before I blow you to kingdom come?"

2

By rights Fargo should have died then and there.

But Harve Koons, in his drunken state, had not pulled the hammers back. When he squeezed the triggers, nothing happened. "What the hell?" he roared, and went to remedy his oversight.

Fargo started to bring the Colt up. He needed to be sure, needed to have the first shot be the last shot. But before the barrel cleared the edge of the table, Lucille Sparks threw herself at Koons. Grabbing the shotgun, she pushed it to one side.

"No, you don't! I won't let you kill him!"

It was just as well the shotgun was not cocked. Had it been, it might have gone off when she jerked on it, doing to her as Koons intended to do to Fargo. But she did gain Fargo the few seconds he needed to dart over and swing his Colt at Koons's temple. His intent was to knock the man out. But just then Koons yanked on the shotgun in an effort to wrest it from Lucille, and in doing so, caused her to stumble—directly into Fargo.

Fargo nearly fell. He tried to straighten but Lucille was clinging to him and her weight sent them stumbling against the table. Swearing, Fargo pushed free of her and spun. The hardwood stock of the shotgun caught him in the gut and he doubled over. The next instant he was staring into its muzzles.

"I have you now!" Koons crowed. But he still had not drawn back the hammers.

Surging erect, Fargo hit him across the right temple,

9

the left temple, and then on the crown of the head. This time when Koons went down, he stayed down.

"Thank God!" the waitress declared.

Fargo sank into a chair. His stomach was a ball of agony. He rested his forearms on his knees and breathed in great gulps until the pain faded. Then, standing and snatching up the shotgun, he thrust it at the waitress. "Take this and hide it in the kitchen."

"But—" the woman began. Something in his eyes silenced her. Nodding, she gingerly grasped it with both hands and hurried toward the back.

Lucille nudged Koons with a toe. "What do we do with this lump of arrogance? Turn him over to Marshal Lewis?"

"He makes a fine rug," Fargo said. But he slid his hands under Koons and dragged him to another table, then hoisted Koons into a chair and placed his head on his arms to give the impression he was asleep. "Let's forget about him and have that coffee."

Instead of sitting across from him, as she had done before, Lucille came and sat next to him. Her elbow brushed his as she leaned forward and said, "That was a bit too much excitement for my taste. Maybe it is a good thing I am heading back to Ohio in the morning."

"What?" This was news to Fargo.

"Didn't I tell you? My parents have been begging me to go back and see them." Lucille shrugged. "I might as well. My personal business here did not turn out as I had hoped." Almost as an afterthought she added, "I leave on the stage at eight."

Fargo hid his disappointment. It was unlikely she would want to stay up half the night when she had to get up early. But he was putting the cart before the horse. "I am sorry to hear that. I was hoping to get better acquainted."

Lucille grinned and looked away. "Yes, it is a shame. I would not mind getting to know you better."

They spent the next hour sipping coffee and talking about everything under the sun. She did most of the talking. Fargo listened and nodded and inserted a word here and there, but mostly he admired her luscious lips and her ripe body and the fragrance of her perfume.

Toward the end of the hour Harve Koons groaned and stirred.

"Just a moment," Fargo said to Lucille. Walking over, he drew his Colt and brought the barrel slashing down. It had the desired effect.

"Oh, my. Did you have to?"

"Do you want him to cause us more trouble?"

Lucille admitted she did not. They finished, paid and walked out. Fargo was pleasantly pleased when she slipped her arm through his. The warm feel of her body made him all the more hungry for her company.

"I must say, I have had a nice time, all things considered. You are quite the gentleman."

"You wouldn't say that if you knew what I was thinking," Fargo said, and winked.

"Oh, my." Lucille grinned. "Direct and to the point. But I am afraid I don't have all my packing done. I really must get ready to leave in the morning. I hope you won't hold it against me."

Fargo was twitching below his belt but it had not reached that point yet. He shook his head.

Her boardinghouse was three blocks from the public square. At the gate to a picket fence she held out her hand and smiled. "I thank you again for an enjoyable evening. Perhaps we will meet again one day."

Fargo waited until she was on the porch and out of earshot before he summed up his sentiments. "Damn." She had put him in the mood for a frolic under the sheets, but it was not meant to be. Turning on a boot heel, he hastened to Bassiter's. The night was young yet. With a little luck he might find a filly who shared his mood. He was almost to the saloon when somewhere behind him a horse whinnied and a man irately bellowed, "Watch where you are going, mister! My horse nearly stepped on you."

Turning, Fargo scanned the street. Two riders, well apart, were coming toward him. He deduced that it was the second rider, half a block away, who had bellowed,

11

and when the horse was almost abreast of him he motioned and said, "Mind my asking what that was all about back there?"

The man had a look of a farmer on his way home. He scowled and replied, "Some damn fool was stalking around with a shotgun. He scooted off when I hollered." With a nod he rode on.

Fargo scanned the street. It had to be Koons. The jackass did not know when to leave well enough alone.

Perhaps a dozen people were moving about. None were Koons, but he could be anywhere, watching from the shadows.

Fargo made too easy a target out in the open. He backpedaled into a gap between the saloon and the building next to it, and palmed his Colt. For long minutes he probed every shadow and doorway. He debated staying put until impatience brought Koons into the open, and decided to hell with it. He was not going to hide like some prairie dog in its burrow. Keeping his eyes on the street, he sidled to the batwings and shouldered on through, twirling the Colt into its holster as he entered.

A blast of sound greeted him: loud voices, lusty laughter, the clink of glasses and the tinkle of chips. A gray-white cloud created by cigar and pipe smoke wreathed the ceiling, its tendrils writhing like snakes. Fargo threaded toward the bar, relaxing a bit more with each stride. Koons could not get a shot at him in there, not without dropping two or three bystanders, and he figured not even Koons was that crazy.

The first glass of whiskey was liquid fire. The second went down smooth. Fargo had the bartender fill his glass a third time and then roved among the tables. He had forty-three dollars in his poke. It wasn't much but it would stake him to a poker game.

An empty chair beckoned. Fargo was in it and sliding his poke from under his buckskin shirt when he noticed a nearby window. Since it faced the public square, which was thronged with people, he deemed it safe to go on sitting there. But he kept an eye on it, just the same.

A half hour later Fargo was over twenty dollars to the better. Three jacks helped. So did a straight. He folded the next hand, then was dealt two kings. He asked for three cards and was given a couple of queens. Two pair was not a great hand but it was good enough to raise. He was so intent on his hand that he did not look up when someone at the next table said, "What in hell does that yack think he is doing?"

The man across from Fargo called his raise. Fargo watched his face, trying to determine if the man was bluffing or had cards worth backing, when another comment caught his attention.

"I don't like how he is waving that shotgun."

Fargo glanced up. Half the people near him were gazing toward the window. Just outside stood a bloodied and battered Harve Koons. Koons looked as if he had been stomped by a bronc. He was peering intently into the saloon, glancing this way and that.

At the same instant that Fargo saw Koons, Koons saw him. Instantly Koons jerked the shotgun to his shoulder. Fargo had underestimated how badly Koons wanted revenge. Witnesses or no witnesses, Harve Koons intended to blow him to hell and back.

"Get down!" a player bawled to no one in particular. "That loon is fixing to shoot!"

Dozens of men dived for the floor. Fargo was one of them. He shoved back his chair and flung himself flat under the table just as the shotgun went off. Glass shattered with a loud crash. A man screamed, and the top of the table drummed to multiple impacts that made Fargo think of hail on a cabin roof. Only this was not hail. It was buckshot.

Women screamed. Men cried out or cursed. Everyone was scrambling for cover.

From under the table, Fargo saw a man thrashing about in pain, one hand on a shoulder oozing blood. The man had been between him and the window and had caught part of the blast meant for Fargo.

Fargo had his Colt out. A thump warned him that Koons had jumped over the sill and was in the saloon.

His hunch was confirmed the next moment when Koons bellowed.

"Drop that, barkeep, or die where you stand!" Apparently the bartender obeyed, because Koons then roared, "Now listen, all of you! I am here for one man and one man only! Stay out of my way or die!"

From over near the far wall came a shout. "You have gone loco, Koons! You will be hung for this!"

"Do you see my face?" Harve Koons raged. "I want the son of a bitch who did this to me! I want him dead and I will have him dead!"

Fargo had not counted on anything like this. When most men were beaten to a pulp, they slunk off to lick their wounds. Not Koons. The beating had brought on a killing madness. Fargo had seen it before. Once, when he was scouting for the army, the patrol he was guiding encountered a Sioux war party. In the clash that ensued, a soldier took an arrow in the shoulder. It drove him mad. The trooper rushed in among the startled Sioux, wielding his empty rifle like a club and laying about him like a lunatic.

"Stand up, you bastard!" Koons shouted. "Stand up and take your medicine!"

Fargo was not about to do any such thing. On his elbows and knees he swiftly crawled past a couple of chairs and under the next table.

"I know where you are!" Koons yelled, his voice sounding closer. "I know exactly where you are! Hiding won't do you any good!"

A .12-gauge was the next best thing to a cannon. All firearms were deadly but a shotgun, specifically a .12-gauge loaded with buckshot, was considered *the* most deadly of all. So deadly, in fact, that there was a popular saying on the frontier to the effect that "buckshot meant burying."

"I won't tell you again! I will count to three and then the dance will commence."

Fargo crawled toward yet another table, passing several men and a woman frozen in fear.

"One!"

"Harve, don't do this!" someone urged.

"Two!"

"Let the rest of these people leave!" a woman shouted. "It's the fellow you are after that you want, not the rest of us."

Koons was distracted from his count. "No one is going anywhere! Anyone tries and they die!"

"You *have* gone loco," said the same man as before. "God help you. The marshal will be here any second."

"Marshal Lewis is out of town, George!" Koons snarled. "Now shut the hell up or you will be next."

By then Fargo had passed a third table and was wriggling like an eel toward a fourth. He had circled as he crawled so that by now he should be somewhere on Koons's left.

"Where was I?" Koons said aloud to himself. "Oh, yeah. I remember." He paused. "Two!"

Fargo did not want more bystanders to take lead meant for him. Accordingly, he heaved up, the Colt at his waist, and fanned off a shot the moment he saw Koons, who happened to look in his general direction just as he rose. He saw Koons jerk to the impact of the slug but it was not enough to drop him.

Harve Koons swung the shotgun in Fargo's direction and unleashed both barrels.

Fargo dropped down a heartbeat before Koons fired. A sizeable chunk of tabletop exploded into bits and pieces, showering him with slivers. He rolled toward another table, or tried to, and collided with a man lying between them. He tried to push the man aside but the man would not budge.

"Where did you get to?"

Koons was coming toward him, undoubtedly reloading as he came. Taking a gamble, Fargo pushed upright, hoping to snap off a shot before Koons could reload. But Koons already had.

Harve Koons sneered in savage glee. That sneer bought Fargo the split-second warning he needed to throw himself flat a fraction of a second before the shotgun went off.

A chair next to Fargo was blown apart. A man screamed. A woman cried out.

Now! Fargo thought, before Koons could reload yet again. He surged to his feet. Harve Koons was frantically extracting a spent shell. Lightning-swift, Fargo banged off three shots. They slammed Koons back, a look of astonishment replacing the rage. A fourth shot drilled Koons through the forehead and snapped his head half around. A fifth was unnecessary but Fargo wanted to be sure.

In the sudden silence, someone coughed.

Relief washed over Fargo. He was about to lower his Colt when something hard was pressed against the nape of his neck and a gun hammer clicked.

"Move and you are dead, mister."

3

Thinking it might be the bartender, Fargo froze. "I didn't start this. You saw for yourself."

"I just got here," the man holding the cocked revolver said. "I want you to hand me your six-shooter. Do it nice and slow or you are liable to end up like Koons."

Fargo balked at being disarmed. "Send for the law. Let them handle this."

"I *am* the law," the man revealed. "Deputy Sheriff Tom Gavin."

A heavyset man in a bowler was rising off the floor. "He is telling the truth, Tom," he said to the deputy. "Koons came crashing through the window like a mad bull."

"Even so," Deputy Gavin said, "I have my duty."

A hand appeared at Fargo's side, palm up.

"I will have your pistol, mister, and I will have it now."

"You want it, it is yours," Fargo said. For the most part he usually abided by the law. But he did not like giving the Colt up. With a sigh he started to raise his arms.

"No need for that," Deputy Gavin said, "if you give me your word you will do as I say and not act up."

"You have it," Fargo said, and turned.

Deputy Gavin had black hair, a cleft chin, and a no-nonsense air about him. Surveying the aftermath, he said bitterly, "That damn fool Koons. Wait for me over by the door."

"How about if I wait at the bar?" Fargo countered. "You are going to be a while."

"That I am," Gavin conceded. "Pour one for me. I will need it by the time I am done."

It took over an hour. The sawbones was sent for to tend the wounded. The undertaker was summoned to cart off the body. Witnesses were quizzed. Upended tables and chairs were set right, and then the debris and the blood were cleaned up.

Through it all, Fargo leaned on an elbow and nursed a glass of whiskey. A few unfriendly glances were thrown his way, suggesting some thought he was partly to blame, but he ignored them. At one point the bartender came over and asked why Koons had been so intent on blowing him to hell and back. Normally, Fargo's personal affairs were just that, but since the bartender was bound to tell all his customers, and in the process clear Fargo of any blame, Fargo told him about his earlier encounters.

A few choice expletives burst from the barkeep. "He was always on the prod, that one." He nodded at the wounded and the cleanup under way. "This was bound to happen sooner or later. I just wish to hell it hadn't happened in my place."

Deputy Gavin was in a somber mood when he led Fargo to the jail. As they were crossing the public square he offhandedly remarked, "Usually Marshal Lewis would handle this but he is taking a prisoner to St. Louis. The sheriff is down sick so that leaves me."

In the office, Gavin bade Fargo sit and asked him to relate his side of events. "Lucy Sparks, you say?" Gavin said when Fargo finished. "I know Miss Sparks. A sweet gal. You wait here while I go have a talk with her."

"Mind if I help myself to some coffee while you are gone?" Fargo asked, nodding at a pot on the stove in the corner.

"Help yourself," Deputy Gavin said, "but I warn you. I made that batch, and it can float a horseshoe."

Fargo had tasted worse. He drank three cups over the next hour, and then the door opened and a tired Deputy

Gavin walked in. Fargo filled a tin cup for him and held it out.

"I'm obliged." Gavin sat behind the desk and propped his boots on the edge. His brow puckered, he took a few sips. "You will be happy to hear that Miss Sparks confirms your story. As near as I can tell this is all on Koons. I have no grounds to hold you."

"I can leave, then?"

"Yes and no. You can leave the jail but I must ask you to stick around town a day or two, in case there are more questions I need to ask."

Fargo frowned.

"I am sorry. I am just doing my job." Deputy Gavin paused. "While I was over talking to Miss Sparks, it hit me. Your name, that is. It is the kind of name people remember. You wouldn't happen to be the same Skye Fargo who was in a shooting match here a while back, would you? The famous scout?"

"I work as a scout sometimes," Fargo said.

"Well, I'll be. The last famous person I met was old Jim Bridger. They say he could track an ant over solid rock. Are you that good?"

"Not quite," Fargo said dryly.

Deputy Gavin chuckled. "At least you are honest. I'll tell you what. I will try my best to get you on your way as soon as I can."

"I appreciate that."

They parted on a friendly note.

Fargo did not have a room for the night. He had left his personal effects with the liveryman, so the stable was his next stop. For a dollar, the man agreed to let him sleep in the hayloft. Fargo spread out his bedroll, placed his holster at his side, and was soon asleep. At the crack of dawn, as was his habit, he awoke. But for once he did not get up. Since he had nowhere to be and nothing to do, he rolled over and went back to sleep.

A ruckus down below woke him a second time. Yawning and stretching, Fargo slowly sat up. Judging by the sunlight flooding the stable through the open double doors, he figured it had to be the middle of the morning, or later. Jamming his hat on his head, he moved to the edge of the loft. Below, several men were hurriedly saddling horses. He was mildly surprised to see that Deputy Tom Gavin was one of them. "Morning, Deputy."

Gavin glanced up, and blinked. "I'll be damned. I was looking all over for you earlier, and here you are."

"Why?" Fargo asked, hoping it did not mean he would be delayed in leaving Springfield.

"It has to do with Miss Sparks," Deputy Gavin said.

"What about her? She told me she was leaving on the eastbound stage this morning," Fargo recollected.

"She did," Gavin confirmed. "She was one of six passengers. The stage was a little past Dawson's Corners, which is about six miles from Springfield as the crow flies, when it happened."

"When what happened?" Fargo prompted when the lawman stopped.

Gavin's features hardened. "Outlaws. The Terrell gang, as they are called. Their leader is Mad Dog Terrell. Name a crime, they have done it. Robbery, murder, rustling, arson."

Fearing the worst, Fargo said, "Did they kill everyone?"

"No. They downed a tree across the road. When the stage stopped, they closed in. The shotgun tried to resist and was shot. The driver threw up his arms but they shot him anyway. They were after the strongbox."

"The passengers?" Fargo prompted.

"They were forced at gunpoint to climb out and hand over their valuables," Deputy Gavin related. "One passenger refused to give up a gold-plated watch and was shot in the foot. Another was clubbed."

"Lucille?"

Deputy Gavin's jaw muscles twitched. "They took her with them. Mad Dog Terrell told the other passengers that she was their guarantee. That if anyone came after them, he would slit her throat."

"Hell," Fargo said.

Deputy Gavin gestured. "I have organized a posse and

we are about to head out. You are welcome to join us. More than welcome since word has it you are one of the best trackers alive. What do you say?"

In his mind's eye Fargo pictured Lucille Sparks, recalling her warmth and friendliness and ready smile. "You can count me in."

They rode out twenty minutes later.

The posse was made up of six men, counting Fargo. Deputy Gavin introduced them.

There was Lynch Spicer, the son of a judge. He favored expensive tailored clothes. His saddle and saddlebags had seen little use, and he rode with a stiff posture that suggested he was more at home in a chair than in the saddle. He had brown hair and green eyes.

Kleb was a bank clerk. His derby and suit were as plain as the man himself. His only distinguishing trait was a short brown mustache, which he kept meticulously trimmed.

A freighter named Foley was also along. Big-boned and brawny, his homespun shirt and pants showed a lot of wear and tear. He had a bushy beard and a sour disposition.

That left Old Charley. None of the others ever called him Charley; it was always Old Charley. His white hair had something to do with it. So did his many wrinkles. But there was nothing old about the lively gleam in his eyes or in the way he moved and swung onto a horse. Old Charley had lived on the frontier nearly all his life, and like Fargo, he wore buckskins, only his had seen a lot more wear and tear. He was fond of tobacco and chewed a wad nonstop.

Aware of the urgency, they pushed their horses as hard as they dared, slowing at intervals so the lathered animals could catch their wind. As it was, the sun was well up in the sky when their destination hove into view.

Fargo had been through the hamlet before but never stopped there. It consisted of a tavern and several cabins situated at a fork in the road. The owner of the tavern, he had heard, was named Dawson, hence Dawson's Corners.

The stage was parked in front of the tavern. A small knot of people were standing about and were quick to gather around the posse. Deputy Gavin shouldered his way inside, leaving Fargo and the others near the hitch rail. Fargo was debating whether to follow him when a hand plucked at his sleeve.

"I am right pleased to have you along, hoss," Old Charley remarked. "These other simpletons don't know the first thing about tracking and such."

"I heard that, old man," Lynch Spicer said. "Watch who you are calling a lunkhead."

"Now, now, sonny." Old Charley grinned. "Just because your pappy is a judge, don't go putting on airs. Old I might be but I can still lick a pup like you any day of the week."

"Can you lick me?" demanded Foley, the freighter, and balled his big fists. "Because if you insult me again, you will have to."

Kleb had removed his derby and was wiping a handkerchief across his balding pate. "Please, gentlemen. Let's not have any bickering. We are in this together, whether we want to be or not."

"How is that?" Fargo asked.

It was Old Charley who answered. "Deputy Gavin came running out of his office and pointing at anyone who happened to be near him, saying you and you and you, follow me. When I asked him what for, he told me I was part of his posse."

"The nerve of him," Lynch Spicer complained. "I have better things to do than go traipsing off after some miscreants."

"Miscre-what?" Old Charley said, and tittered. "Hell, boy, why do you always use those fifty-cent words?"

"You could have refused," Fargo said to Spicer.

Lynch snorted and shook his head. "You don't know my father, Judge Thaddeus Spicer. If he found out I shirked my civic duty, he would withhold my allowance for a month to punish me."

"And young Mr. Spicer needs that money for the ladies and the gaming tables," Old Charley teased. "If his pappy ever tightened the purse strings, this boy wouldn't know what to do with himself."

"You go to hell," Lynch said.

Old Charley cackled. "That's the trouble with this world. Too many folks take offense when they shouldn't."

"The trouble with this world," Foley interjected, "is jackasses like you who reckon they can go around insulting folks and not have those they insult get riled."

Kleb, in the act of placing his derby back on his head, said loudly, "Here we go again. Can't you please get along?"

"I might have to be here but I don't have to like it— or you," Lynch Spicer declared.

"You and me feel the same, papa's boy," Foley said.

Lynch bristled and straightened. "Don't call me that."

"Or what?" Foley taunted. "You will throw a tantrum? Because if you lift a hand to me, I will by God break it off."

"Wonderful," Kleb muttered. "This is just wonderful."

Fargo was inclined to agree. As a posse they would make a great bunch of barroom brawlers. Disgusted, he turned to go in the tavern. A man with his arm in a sling was just coming out, and at sight of him, the man broke into a grin.

"Skye Fargo, as I live and breathe!"

Fargo shook the callused hand thrust at him. "Ben Weaver, you ornery cuss. How have you been?" Weaver had been driving stages for as long as Fargo could remember. Not quite as ancient as Old Charley, Weaver's features were bronzed by constant exposure to the sun and seamed from the elements.

"I was doing right fine until Mad Dog Terrell went and shot me." Weaver indicated his wounded shoulder. "Damn him to hell, anyway. I didn't give him cause." He glanced at the men by the hitch rail. "Say, are you part of the posse that is going out after those polecats?"

Fargo nodded.

"That gal must have been born under a lucky star," Weaver said. "With you along they are as good as caught."

Fargo did not see anything lucky about being in the clutches of cutthroats. "What can you tell me about Terrell and those with him?"

Weaver's grin evaporated. "They are as ruthless a bunch as ever drew breath. For five or six years now they have been doing as they damn well please, killing and raping and whatnot. There are four of them." He held up a finger as he mentioned each one. "A breed named Yoas, a gent out of New Orleans or thereabouts called DePue, a hard case with the handle of Mattox, and Mad Dog Terrell himself. His nickname says it all. He's rabid, that one, vicious to the bone." Weaver looked Fargo in the eyes. "You be careful, pard. Real careful. If you're not, any one of those curly wolves will kill you dead as dead can be."

4

Fargo expected the posse to head out right away, so he was considerably surprised when Deputy Gavin came out of the tavern to announce, "We will stay the night and leave first thing in the morning."

Kleb, of all people, gave voice to Fargo's thoughts. "What in God's name for? Who knows what those vermin will do to that poor girl? We should mount up right this moment."

"In the first place, I make the decisions, not you," Deputy Gavin responded. "In the second place, we are waiting for another posse member who knows the country the outlaws are heading into. I sent a rider to fetch the man we need and he should be here by ten tonight at the very latest. It will be too dark to track by then, so we might as well wait until morning."

"Why not go on anyway and have this other hombre catch up?" Foley rumbled.

"And risk having him not find us?" Deputy Gavin rejoined. "I repeat. He knows the country better than any of us. His family lived in the mountains to the south for years and only moved up this way about nine months ago." Gavin looked at Fargo. "We can still use an expert tracker, though, so I hope you stay with us."

Thinking of Lucille Sparks, Fargo replied, "I will stick until the finish." He did not like to think of what that might be.

As the lawman went back inside, Lynch Spicer remarked, "I wonder who he has sent for."

"I might have an idea," Old Charley said. "There's a family by the name of Jentry, a backwoods clan who used to live south of here. Could be he sent for one of them."

"I bet that is it," Ben Weaver agreed. "But it could be he sent that rider for nothing."

"How do you mean?" Fargo asked.

"The Jentrys don't like outsiders. They keep to themselves and like it that way."

Fargo had met their kind before. Hill folk, as hard and as tough as the land they wrested a living from, they wanted nothing to do with the rest of the world. "Let's hope whoever it is shows up." Otherwise, they would waste precious time better spent dogging the Terrell gang.

"Well, since you aren't going anywhere, how about if you let me buy you a drink and then take your money at cards?" Weaver proposed with a mischievous chuckle.

Old Charley piped up with, "Sounds fine to me. There is nothing I hate worse than sitting around doing nothing."

Fargo was not fond of it himself. They went in to find the tavern busier than it would normally be. The stage passengers were still there, being questioned by Deputy Gavin, and the residents of Dawson's Corners were there as well, along with a few local farmers.

Fargo selected a corner table and bellowed for a bottle. No sooner had he sat in a chair facing the door than perfume wreathed him in a fragrant cloud and a slender hand set a whiskey bottle in front of him.

"Anything else, handsome?"

Fargo looked up. She was tall, almost as tall as he was, with a lean, curvy build and long, willowy legs that seemed to go on forever under a form-hugging homespun dress and an apron. Her shoulder-length sandy hair contrasted nicely with her blue eyes. "You're the bartender?"

"I will go you one better. I own the place. Ira Dawson, at your service." She smiled as she said it, and placed her hand on his shoulder.

26

Was she staking a claim? Fargo wondered. "Somehow I had the idea it was run by a man."

"It was, by my husband, until he up and died on me," Ira said. "His heart gave way just like that." She snapped her fingers. "And him in the prime of his life and never sick a day."

Old Charley stopped chomping on his tobacco to say, "That happens sometimes, ma'am. I've known folks who I would have sworn were fit as fiddles, yet they keeled over the same as some who have consumption. When it's our time to go, the good Lord takes us whether we are healthy or not."

"That's an interesting way of looking at it," Ben Weaver said. "Me, I have so many creaking joints and aches, it wouldn't surprise me if this worn-out body of mine went any day now."

Ira Dawson had not taken her hand off Fargo. He smiled up at her and asked, "Do you serve eats as well as drink?"

"That I do, but not until supper time. Although for you I am willing to make an exception."

"That's hospitable of you."

Ira's fingers gently squeezed. "When I see someone I like, I can be as hospitable as can be."

Old Charley snorted, and Ira turned on him.

"You will remember I am a lady, you old goat, or I will have you tossed out on your ear."

"No offense intended, ma'am," the old frontiersman assured her. "There was a time when I was as hospitable toward ladies as you are toward handsome gents. But that was ages ago, I am sorry to say, when I was young and good-looking. Nowadays, my wrinkles tend to scare the women off."

"Either that, or those brown teeth of yours," Ira said, and swished off toward the bar.

"Fine figure of a female, there," Weaver commented. "But I was led to believe she has not shared her bed since her husband died." He looked at Fargo. "How do you do it?"

"Do what?"

"Play innocent, why don't you?" the stage driver bantered. "But I have known you a good long while, and I have seen how the females hop right in your lap. How do you do it? What is the secret?"

"He is young and he is handsome," Old Charley said. "It is no great mystery why mares are attracted to stallions."

"You don't understand," Ben Weaver said. "You have not been around him as often as I have. We could be in a place with a hundred other men, and the prettiest gal there will make a beeline for Fargo, here, before any of the others."

"You're exaggerating," Fargo said.

"Not by much. Most men would give anything to have half the luck you do," Weaver asserted.

"Back in my day the ladies loved to sit in my lap, too," Old Charley claimed. "I helped things along by rubbing bear fat all over me."

"Bear fat?" Weaver repeated in disbelief.

"Sure. A lot of Indians use it in their hair and the Indian girls all like it, so I rubbed it all over to give me twice the smell."

"I don't think bear fat would work with white women," Weaver said. "Hog fat, maybe, since it's kind of sweet smelling except when it has turned rancid." He shifted toward Fargo and sniffed. "Is that your secret?"

"I like raccoon fat, myself," Fargo said, trying to keep a straight face.

"If there is no fat handy, I recommend strawberry juice," Old Charley suggested. "You crush the strawberries and smear the juice on your face so you smell just like one."

"I never thought of that," Ben Weaver said. "But doesn't it make your face all pink?"

"Sure. But women like pink. The pinker you are, the more they can't wait to get their lips on you."

"You don't say," Weaver said.

Fargo laughed.

"What tickled your funny bone?" Old Charley asked.

"The only fat around here is the fat between certain ears."

The rest of the afternoon was spent playing poker and drinking. The delay did not sit well with Fargo. At one point he went over to where Deputy Gavin was talking to a passenger who had been relieved of all his valuables. Fargo offered to go on alone and blaze a trail for them to follow.

"I like the idea," Gavin admitted. "But there is always the chance we will miss the marks. You could wind up tangling with Terrell and his hellions all by your lonesome."

"I don't mind the odds."

"I admire your grit but I would rather not run the risk."

"It is my risk to take," Fargo said, thinking of Lucille Sparks.

"True," the deputy allowed. "But I will be held responsible if anything happens to you."

Fargo spent another ten minutes trying to persuade him, to no avail. He went back to his whiskey and his cards, but he was not happy about it. The more he dwelled on the idea of Lucy in the hands of men who would have their way with her as quick as look at her, the less he liked sitting on his backside while the clock over the bar ticked away the time the posse was wasting. "All I can say," he remarked late in the afternoon, "is that whoever Gavin sent for better be damn worth the wait."

"I had me the same notion," Old Charley mentioned. "My ma always said no dawdling in the outhouse, and I took it to heart."

Kleb, who was sitting in on the game now, scratched his chin in puzzlement. "This is a tavern, not an outhouse. I don't see how your mother's words of wisdom apply."

"You will when you are my age," was Old Charley's retort.

Lynch Spicer, Fargo observed, had glued his elbows to

the bar and kept trying to get Ira Dawson to chat with him. She wouldn't give him so much as a friendly smile, which seemed to annoy him.

At the far end, moodily drinking alone, was Foley. Whenever anyone went over to him he made it plain he did not care for company.

"What put a burr up his backside?" Ben Weaver wondered after the big freighter had told a farmer to go pester someone else.

"Foley?" Kleb said. "He has always been a grump, for as long as I have known him."

"Some folks are born bitter and stay that way," Old Charley said.

"I hear he lost his family a while back," Kleb enlightened them. "Something to do with he took it into his head to head for Oregon alone. He made it over South Pass, the story goes, and one day went off to hunt for their supper pot. When he came back to the wagon, they had all been massacred. His wife, two daughters and a son."

"Hell," Ben Weaver said.

"So I can't say I blame him for being as he is," Kleb went on. "If I had a wife and kids I wouldn't like to lose them, either."

"It was his own fault," Old Charley declared. "Only a blamed fool tries to make it through hostile country alone."

Fargo agreed. Foley would have been wiser to join a wagon train. But some men expected calamities to befall others. They thought they were immune, that they could go through life without a lick of common sense and not reap the consequences. Live and learn, Fargo reflected.

Along about seven in the evening the stage was permitted to leave. As the eager passengers climbed in, Weaver swung up onto the seat.

"Are you sure you don't want someone else to take it out?" Deputy Gavin asked. "With your hurt wing, and all?"

"I still have one good arm," Ben Weaver replied. "Besides, I have been doing this so long, I could do it in my sleep. I'll be fine."

"Suit yourself." Deputy Gavin closed the stagecoach door and patted it. "You are ready to roll."

Weaver grinned down at Fargo. "You be careful. I don't want to hear that Mad Dog Terrell made a poke out of your skin." He hollered, "Get along, there!" at the team, and wheeled the stage out of there as smoothly as if he had the use of both hands.

"Would Terrell really do that?" Kleb asked as the dust the stagecoach raised swirled about them.

"Skin a man?" Old Charley said. "Hell, haven't you heard? The things he's done make an Apache seem tame. He cuts off fingers, he cuts off toes. He's partial to ears, too, they say. Once he gutted a man and dragged him by his intestines."

Kleb had turned a shade of green. "Surely not."

"It is all true, I am afraid," Deputy Gavin said. "Which is why we are not taking any chances we do not have to take. We will do this right and come out of it alive."

"I am all for being alive," Old Charley said. "When you get my age, you savor life more."

"Where is that Jentry you sent for?" Foley asked the lawman. "Shouldn't he have been here by now?"

"It could be a while yet," Gavin said. "The man I sent only had a general idea where to find their cabin."

"Then why send him?"

"Because he was the only one who had any idea at all." Gavin gazed at the thick woodland to the north. "The Jentrys discourage visitors. I doubt there is a soul in all of Springfield who has ever been to their place."

"If they are that unsociable," Kleb said, "what makes you think they will agree to help?"

"It is worth a try," Gavin insisted. "They know the country."

Fargo turned to go back in and was once again enveloped by musky perfume. Ira Dawson had a shawl over her shoulders and was fluffing her hair.

"Here you are. I usually take an hour or so off about this time of day and let my helper handle the bar. How about if we go for a stroll?"

Old Charley snickered.

"Do that again," Ira said, "and I will shove a darning needle so far up your hind end, it will come out your nose."

"Ouch," Old Charley said.

Ira faced Fargo. "Well? Would you care to stretch your legs or not?"

Fargo's gaze roved from her hair to her bosom to the curve of her hips, and lower down. "I like to stretch legs," he said.

5

Forest hemmed the hamlet. The sun, poised on the rim of the world, bathed the timber in a rosy glow. Birds warbled and chirped, squirrels scampered for their nests, and now and again the eternal question of an early-rising owl went unanswered.

Ira Dawson led Fargo around behind her tavern and along a well-worn footpath that wound among the oaks, maples and elms. "I like to go for a walk at this time of day," she remarked. "It relaxes me."

Fargo breathed deep of the dank forest odor. He was more at home in the wilds, in certain respects, than among the stone and brick byways of man. "It is nice here," he said for lack of anything else to say.

"Dawson's Corners might seem no-account to some," Ira said. "It is small and it is quiet and not much ever goes on, but I like it that way. I can do without the hustle and bustle of a city, and I prefer my humanity in small doses."

Fargo shared her outlook, to a degree. There was only so much civilized society he could abide before he had to take himself to parts unknown to remind himself what it was like to be as free as the birds singing in the trees. "Do you ever aim to remarry?"

Ira shrugged. "Who can predict? I loved my Orville. He was not the brightest candle in the world but he was devoted to me and that counts for more as far as I am concerned." She slowed and loosened her shawl. "He could be a trial, though, like most men. He would slack

33

off at his work, and that vexed me, or he would forget to do something I asked, and that vexed me. I am in no hurry to hitch myself to more vexation, thank you very much."

Fargo grinned. "I like how you come right out and say what is on your mind."

"Oh pshaw. I am not green behind the ears. I know what life has to offer, and what it can take away, and I won't waste my time or yours beating around the bush when every minute is so precious." Ira smiled and clasped his hand. "I hope you won't think it brazen of me."

They passed under a spreading bough and a tanager took flight, a burst of color against the green.

"It wouldn't hurt if more women were like you," Fargo remarked.

Ira cocked her head at him. "You can't blame my gender for being wary. A dalliance can cost us a lot more than it ever costs a man. We are the ones who grow heavy with child. We are the ones who give birth. You men have it easy. You can poke when and where you will and go your merry way and never fret that your desire will create new life in you."

"That's true," Fargo said. "If you are having second thoughts—"

"Did I say that?" Ira cut him off. "I was speaking of womankind in general. Me, I can't have babies. Orville and me tried and tried and finally I went to the doctor, and after the sawbones examined parts of me no one had ever seen but my husband, he told us we could try until the world ended and we would never have children." She paused. "Orville, bless him, said it didn't matter, even though I could tell it did. And now he is gone." Her eyes misted and she fell silent.

Fargo was worried his question had spoiled her mood. "Sorry if I upset you," he said.

"Not at all. These tears aren't sad tears. They are love tears. Orville was a dunce sometimes but he was my dunce and he had my heart in his hands, and there are moments, like now, when I miss him almost more than

34

I can bear." Ira coughed and dabbed at her eyes with her sleeve, then brightened. "There. See? All better."

"I must say, I am flattered," Fargo sought to change the subject.

"You should be," Ira said. "You are only the second since Orville passed on. The first was a gambler who was passing through on the stage. I took a shine to him and told him that if he ever passed this way again, he should consider staying longer. Damn me if he didn't show up late that very night after riding the horse he rented in Springfield near to death."

"Lucky gambler," Fargo said.

By then they were a goodly distance from the hamlet. Ira stopped and faced him and her lips curled in invitation. "I reckon this is far enough. No one hardly ever strays out here. They are too afeared of bears and Injuns and such."

"And you aren't?"

"The only bears we have are black bears, and a loud hoot and holler usually sends them running. The last hostile Injun was killed in these parts pretty near ten years ago."

"There are always those like Mad Dog Terrell and his breed," Fargo mentioned.

"What would he want with me when he helps himself to pretty young things like I hear this Miss Sparks is?"

"You are not that old."

"And you, handsome, can talk a girl to death." Ira pressed against him, her bosom flush with his chest, her face upturned so their mouths were inches apart. "I did not come out here to gab. If you did, then you are not the lady-killer that twinkle in your eyes says you are."

"I twinkle?" Fargo teased.

"Damn. Do you ever shut up?"

Fargo's laugh was smothered by her warm lips. She kissed him hard, almost fiercely, as if unleashing passion she had long pent up. Her tongue darted out and entwined with his as her hands roved up his arms to his shoulders. The kiss went on and on and only ended when Ira stepped back, her eyelids hooded.

"Whew! That was nice. You *can* do more than talk. For a bit there you had me worried."

"Now who is doing too much talking?" Fargo pulled her to him and locked mouths. He kneaded her bottom and her lower back, then drifted one hand high while the other went low. She squirmed and wriggled in growing arousal, her breath as hot as fire.

"That was *really* nice. You are some kisser. Better than Orville. He tried his best, but when he used his hands he would forget what his mouth was supposed to do, and when he was kissing me, his hands just hung there. It always amazed me he could chew food and talk at the same time."

"Speaking of talking," Fargo said, and kissed her again. This time he pried at the tiny buttons and stays on her dress and soon had it down around her elbows. She had gorgeous breasts, full and round. Slipping a hand under, he pinched first one nipple and then the other and was rewarded with a shudder and a lusty groan.

"You put poor Orville to shame. Compared to you, he was a tree stump."

Fargo was tired of hearing about her husband. He nipped her earlobe, licked her neck, ran his tongue along her jaw and up to her mouth where her tongue greeted his. Both of her breasts were now exposed, their nipples as rigid as tacks. Bending slightly, he sucked on one, causing her to gasp and arch her back.

"Oh, my! You do that marvelously well."

Switching to the other nipple, Fargo squeezed and massaged while rubbing his leg against hers. He slid his knee as high up as her thighs, and she ground into him. When she opened her mouth to say something, he covered it with his.

The setting sun, the sounds of the woods, all faded into the background. All Fargo saw was her luscious body. All he heard were her coos and moans. She was having an effect on him, too; his member was iron hard and bulging fit to burst from his buckskin britches. He happened to glance down and saw her reach for him, stop, then reach for him again, and stop again. For all her yearning she was timid at heart so he helped her out. He covered her hand with his and placed her hand on his manhood.

"Goodness gracious! You really do put Orville to shame," Ira whispered, her wide eyes glued to his bulge. Her amazement did not stop her from fondling him, slowly, almost fearfully at first, and then with rising ardor. In her excitement she squeezed a little too hard more than once, causing Fargo to wince. About the fourth time he warned, only half in jest, "Be careful you don't break it."

"What?"

"It is not a stick," Fargo said gruffly.

After that Ira took more care, and while she exercised her fascination with him, he explored her. She was not as full-bodied as some women he had been with but she was wonderfully winsome, and then there were those long, willowy legs of hers. He devoted a lot of caressing and kisses to her thighs, and the more he did, the more aroused she became.

Eventually came the moment when Fargo had her on her back on the ground and he was on his knees. He rubbed the tip of his pole along her moist slit and a delicious shiver ran through her. She had stopped talking, thank God, and was overcome with passion.

Fargo slowly penetrated her. He slowly rocked back and forth, thrusting in and out, her long legs wrapped around him. Their explosion was mutual. Fargo held off until she stiffened and cried out, then gave rein to his own release.

Spent, they lay side by side, Ira's cheek on Fargo's shoulder, her hand on his chest. He looked down and, despite the spreading twilight, noticed wet streaks on her cheeks.

"You're crying?"

"Sorry," Ira said, and sniffled.

"Did I hurt you?"

"Oh, no, no, no." Ira smiled and kissed his neck. "You

were wonderful. Everything I had always hoped my Orville would be. I am grateful, is all. Grateful for meeting you, grateful for this."

Fargo was sorry he got her talking again. "Why don't we rest a bit and head back?" He hitched at his pants and adjusted his buckskins and gun belt so they were as they should be, then he placed an arm behind his head for a pillow, and was set to doze off when he happened to glance at the surrounding woods. He would never know what made him do it. His normally keen senses had been blunted by the lethargy he invariably felt afterward. But he did look, and it was well for him and for her that he did.

For a few seconds the figure hunched in the undergrowth seemed to be just another shadow. Then it moved, and Fargo caught the dull glint of metal. Instinct took over. The figure was to the south, not to the west as it would be if it were someone from Dawson's Corners. That the person was crouched low, and had a gun, and had gone to the trouble to slink close, decided Fargo's course of action. Bellowing "Look out!" he rolled to the left, taking Ira with him. She squawked in surprise just as a pistol went off and a lead slug thudded into the earth in the very spot they had occupied.

Fargo kept on rolling. They were not far from heavy brush. Another shot boomed but again the would-be killer missed. The moment they were in waist-high growth, he let go of her and sprang up into a crouch, drawing the Colt as he rose.

The would-be killer had decided two misses were enough and was racing to the south.

Rising and giving chase, Fargo banged off a shot of his own. It did not seem to have any effect. He blamed the intervening trees. There were too damn many. He ran faster and saw a face glance back. It was a man. That much he could tell. But not the details of hair color or eyes or features. A small man, and god-awful fast. The assassin began to widen his lead.

Fargo was not accustomed to being outrun. He was considered fleet of foot, but the man he was after was faster. That galled him more than almost being taken by surprise. Had he not glanced at the vegetation when he did, there was no doubt in his mind that he or Ira or both would be dead.

Gritting his teeth, Fargo tapped into his last iota of energy. He and the small man both were thrashing through the vegetation heedless of the noise they made. Presently a large silhouette ahead of the man made his escape almost certain. The shape whinnied.

"Damn!" Fargo growled. In frustration he snapped off another shot. It, too, proved a waste of lead.

Then the man was at his mount and vaulted onto it without breaking stride. Bent low over the saddle, he wheeled the horse and used his spurs, and off the animal galloped.

Fargo stopped. He tried for a shot but again the trees thwarted him. Mad enough to spit nails, he jerked the Colt down and indulged in more swearing. Behind him a foot crunched. He whirled, set to fan the Colt, but caught himself in time.

"Who was it?" Ira excitedly asked. "Did you get a look at him?" She scoured the woods ahead but the rider had already melted into the vegetation. "Was that a horse I heard? Why would anyone shoot at us?"

"Your guess is as good as mine," Fargo answered. He had no idea at all.

"It makes no sense," Ira declared. "Were they after you or were they after me?"

"You tell me and we will both know."

"I can't think of a soul who would want me dead," Ira prattled on. "I don't have any enemies. It certainly can't be anyone from the tavern. They are all friends and acquaintances, or members of the posse."

"Let's head back," Fargo proposed. The shots were bound to have been heard and someone was sure to investigate.

They had gone halfway when Deputy Gavin and Old Charley came running toward them with their revolvers out.

"What is going on?" the lawman wanted to know. "We heard shots, and I noticed you were missing."

"We were out for a walk," Fargo said, and almost grinned when Ira blushed. "Someone tried to back-shoot us."

Old Charley spat tobacco juice, then wiped his mouth with his sleeve. "Any polecat who will shoot a female is as low as they come."

"What I want to know," Deputy Gavin said, "is the who and the why."

"That makes two of us," Fargo said as they fell into step on either side.

"Do you think we can catch him quick if we get to our horses and head right out?" Gavin asked.

"No," Fargo admitted. Soon it would be too dark to track unless he used a torch, and men who held torches were easy to put lead into. "We might as well wait for daylight."

"Saving Miss Sparks comes first," Deputy Gavin said.

"Provided she is still alive," Old Charley noted.

"That will be enough of that kind of talk," Ira scolded him.

Deputy Gavin shoved his revolver into his holster. "This does not bode well," he commented. "It does not bode well at all."

6

The whiskey burned down Fargo's throat to his belly and welcome warmth spread all through him. He set the bottle on the bar, smiled and said, "Thanks. Are you sure I can't pay you?"

"It is on the house," Ira said from the other side of the counter, and winked. "I would say you earned it, wouldn't you?"

Fargo chuckled and treated himself to another swallow. They had been back only a few minutes. Deputy Gavin was over at a table with the rest of the posse. Locals were playing cards or nursing drinks.

Night had fallen. A moonless, muggy Missouri night, with crickets chirping and an occasional coyote imitating his prairie brethren.

Fargo was about to take another chug when he realized he had neglected to replace the spent cartridges in his Colt. Annoyed at himself for the lapse, he promptly did so. He was replacing the last one when hooves drummed outside.

Everyone was suddenly interested in the front door. In came a squat man in town clothes thick with dust. He wore a bowler, which he removed and used to swat at his clothes, oblivious to the stares of the patrons.

"Frank!" Deputy Gavin exclaimed, and came out of his chair in a rush to clap the man on the arms. "Why are you alone? Did you find them? Did you relay my message?"

"One at a time," Frank said, replacing his bowler.

"Yes, I found their cabin, but it took a lot of doing. They are so far back in the woods, they might as well be in the next state. If the doc hadn't given us instructions on how to get there—"

"Yes, yes," Gavin cut him off. "But why didn't one of them come back with you?"

"I told them exactly what you told me to say," Frank reported. "I spoke to the father, to Rufus Jentry himself. I said that you wanted him or one of his sons to serve on your posse."

"And?"

"He refused," Frank said. "And before you say anything, yes, I told him it was official, and that you had the legal right to get a posse up, and it was their duty as citizens to lend a hand. All the stuff you told me to say, I said. But it didn't do any good."

Deputy Gavin did not hide his disappointment. "What excuse did he give for not helping?"

"Let's see if I can remember his exact words," Frank said, and then quoted, "We don't have no truck with the outside world and the outside world don't have none with us. There is no law that says a body has to join a posse if they don't want to. So go back and tell your law dog that the Jentrys do not do dog work."

"He said that? He called it dog work?"

Frank nodded. "I wasn't about to argue. There must be twenty of those Jentrys, and they were eyeing me like I was a turkey and they were starved."

"Thanks for trying," Deputy Gavin said. "I don't hold it against you that you failed."

"I never said that," Frank responded, and a strange expression came over him. "I did, in fact, bring a Jentry with me."

"But you just said the father refused to help."

"The father did, and the sons did, and—" Frank stopped, and rather sheepishly grinned. "Here. See for yourself." He turned and gave a shout. "You can come in now if you want."

In the hush that fell when the door opened, Fargo could have heard a feather flutter to the floor.

42

In came a woman. But what a woman. She had to be in her twenties, with tawny hair and blue eyes and full lips. She had the kind of body that made men drool. In short, she was all female, but there was nothing womanly about the men's clothes she wore, or her boots, or the pistol and knife at her hip and the rifle cradled in her arm. Tanned from the sun, lithe and graceful when she moved, she resembled nothing so much as a two-legged cougar.

"Deputy Gavin," Frank said, "I would like you to meet Bobbie Joe Jentry. She is Rufus's daughter."

"What is she doing here?" Gavin asked.

"I can answer for myself," Bobbie Joe Jentry said. "But I should think it would be as plain as the nose on your face. I came to do what my kin will not. I came to join your posse."

Gavin was speechless. A few of the locals looked at one another and grinned. Foley laughed out loud and declared, "If this don't beat all."

Bobbie Joe Jentry walked over, looked the big freighter right in the eyes and said, "Care to explain that?"

"A woman on a posse!" Foley said. "Who ever heard of such a thing? Go back home, girl, and tend to your cooking and knitting."

Before anyone could so much as blink, the muzzle of Bobbie Joe's rifle was an inch from Foley's big nose. "I don't knit. I don't cook. I hunt what goes in the pot. I am better in the woods than you any day. And if you take that tone with me again, you bleed."

Foley had more bluster than sense. "Are you threatening me, girl? I ought to take you over my knee and tar the living daylights out of you."

Everyone heard the hammer click. "Why don't you try?" Bobbie Joe said sweetly. "I haven't shot any idiots in a while and I can use the practice."

Deputy Gavin found his voice. "Here now," he said, hurrying over. "We will have none of that, young lady. You can't go around shooting people. It is against the law."

"I am my own law," Bobbie Joe said. But she let down

the hammer and lowered her rifle. "Are you as pig-headed as he is? Or do you still want help?"

"I didn't expect a woman to come," Gavin said.

"I am the equal of any man. I have lived in the woods all my life, and I am the best hunter in my family. Frank, there, said you need someone who knows the mountains south of here and I know that country like I know the back of my hand."

"But it doesn't seem right," Deputy Gavin said uncertainly.

Fargo had his back to the bar and was indulging in more red-eye. He could not help but notice the twin peaks that thrust against her shirt, or the contours of her hips and legs. "Let her come," he said. "She can be of help."

Gavin and Bobbie Joe both looked at him, and the deputy said, "But what if she comes to harm? I don't want that on my conscience."

"It could happen to any of us," Fargo said. "We know what we are in for. So does she, I reckon."

"Thanks, stranger," Bobbie Joe said. "Who might you be?"

Fargo told her.

"I thought so," Bobbie Joe said. "I saw you once, over to Springfield, when they held that shootin' contest. My whole family came. My pa wanted to see Buck Smith, the buffalo hunter, and I had heard Dottie Wheatridge was takin' part. There was Vin Chadwell, too, as I recollect. And you." She smiled at the memory. "Lord almighty, there was some glorious shootin' that day! I hate to admit it, but they could shoot better than me, and that takes some doin'."

"Maybe so," Fargo said, "but Buck Smith wasn't half as pretty."

Bobbie Joe Jentry had nice teeth. "I asked around about you, and folks say that as good as you are at shootin', you are even better at trackin', and as good as you are at trackin', you are even better at beddin' women. Is that true?"

Her bluntness caught Fargo off guard. He felt his ears grow warm at the laughter that broke out, and caught Ira staring hard at him. "You shouldn't believe everything you hear, girl."

"I am a woman, thank you very much," Bobbie Joe corrected him.

That she was, Fargo had to admit, all woman from head to toe. "I will drink to that," he said, and did so.

Bobbie Joe turned back to Gavin. "Well, mister law, what do you say? Can you use my help or not?"

"I can, yes, but—"

Holding up a hand, Bobbie Joe said, "Stop right there. You strike me as decent enough, and your worry is genuine, but I am full grown, and I can do as I please. It pleases me to help you hunt down Mad Dog Terrell and his pack of wolves. If you have any brains between those ears, you will accept my offer."

"I like her," Old Charley said.

"I don't," Foley threw out.

Lynch Spicer was looking at her as if she were a ripe peach he wanted to take a bite out of, while Kleb appeared bored.

Deputy Gavin drew himself up to his full height. "Very well. I accept. But there are rules you must follow."

"What kind of rules?"

"I am in charge. You are to do as I say. We want to catch Terrell and his men, yes, but not at the cost of our lives. Above all, we want to rescue the hostage they hold, a Miss Lucille Sparks."

"They took a woman?" Bobbie Joe said. "Your man didn't mention that."

Frank had been listening to the whole exchange, and now he stepped forward. "If it is all the same to you, Tom, I will head back to Springfield. I have done as you wanted, and I have a wife and supper waiting."

"Off you go then. I will walk you out."

Fargo turned to the bar and smiled at Ira but she did not return it. He chuckled and was raising the bottle when an arm brushed his.

"I want to thank you again for stickin' up for me."

"I just hope my doing so doesn't get you killed," Fargo said, and took another swallow.

Bobbie Joe Jentry held out a hand. "May I?"

Fargo looked on in wonder as her throat bobbed several times. She neither coughed nor blinked. "Damn. Where did you learn to drink like that?"

"From my pa. He makes his own. This stuff is water compared to his." Grinning, Bobbie Joe gave the bottle back.

"You hunt and you drink. Now tell me you do the other and I will say I am in love," Fargo teased her.

"If by 'other' you mean what I think you do," Bobbie Joe responded, "I would say all that talk about your petticoat chasin' is true."

"You aren't wearing a skirt," Fargo noted.

"I am glad I am not. If I were, your hand would probably be halfway up it and I would have to cut your hand off." Bobbie Joe patted her knife.

Fargo laughed heartily. She was a woman after his own heart. "To the day you wear one," he said, and tipped the bottle.

"To the day I cut off that hand," Bobbie Joe retorted, and took the whiskey from him.

Deep inside of Fargo, something stirred. An emotion he had not felt in so long, he had almost forgotten what it felt like. "Do you have yourself a man, Bobbie Joe Jentry?"

She glanced at him sharply, then tempered the glance with a smile. "I do declare. I believe you are interested."

"I was curious, is all," Fargo said.

"That's funny. You don't look like a cat."

Her laugh was low and deep but not mocking, and Fargo hid his reaction by chugging more whiskey. She was studying him; he refused to look at her. When Ira came sidling along the bar, he was almost grateful.

"It is nice to see you two getting along so well. How are you, Bobbie Joe? The last time I saw you was, what, six months ago when you stopped by with your father and mother?"

"How do you do, Ira," Bobbie Joe said, holding out her hand to shake as a man would. "Five months, more like. You were awful nice to us, putting us up for the night and all."

"It was my pleasure, my dear," Ira assured her. "If there is anything I can get you, just give a holler." She went off to serve another customer.

Bobbie Joe's brow furrowed and she looked from Fargo to Ira and back again. "You are a wonderment."

"Drinking red-eye is no great feat," Fargo said.

"I am talkin' about her." Bobbie Joe nodded toward Ira's back. "How did you get her to make love to you?"

Fargo nearly choked on the whiskey he was downing. Coughing, he wiped his mouth and regarded her with some astonishment. "What makes you think she did?"

"I could see it in her eyes, in how she looked at you," Bobbie Joe said. "How long have you known her?"

"Since earlier today." Fargo continued to be impressed. "Tell me. Do you read sign as well as you read people?"

"Better."

"Good. Having two trackers on this posse increases the odds of us making it in and out alive."

"I intend to live," Bobbie Joe said. "And it won't bother me a lick if I have to kill some of those outlaws, neither."

Deputy Gavin joined them. Stifling a yawn, he announced, "We leave at first light. Feel free to do whatever you like until then, although I advise you to turn in early. You will need your rest."

Out of the blue, Bobbie Joe Jentry remarked, "I have met Terrell, you know."

"No, I did not," Deputy Gavin said. "When?"

"A few months ago. My whole family went to a lake to fish and frolic, and him and his men happened by. They didn't try to harm us. Too many of us, I reckon, with too many rifles."

"What can you tell me about him that I don't already know? Something that might help us bring him to bay?"

"The only thing you need to know about Mad Dog

47

Terrell," Bobbie Jo Jentry said, "is that they don't call him Mad Dog for nothin'."

"That is not much help," Deputy Gavin said.

"Then how about this. The men he rides with, Yoas and DePue and Mattox? They all have cold eyes, the coldest I ever saw. I don't scare easy but bein' around them made me nervous."

Fargo thought of poor Lucy Sparks.

As if she were privy to his thoughts, Bobbie Joe said, "Whoever that gal is they took, she would be better off dead."

7

Before the sun was up they were saddling their mounts. Kleb asked Deputy Gavin if they were bringing a pack-horse and Gavin replied that they would travel fast and light and live off the land as they went. Kleb did not seem all that pleased by the news.

Fargo and Bobbie Joe Jentry were ready to go before the others. As they sat their horses, waiting, she shifted in the saddle and smiled.

"This should be fun."

"As bad as you make Terrell and his men out to be, there is a good chance some of us won't make it back alive. You call that fun?"

"The hunt will be," Bobbie Joe said, a fierce gleam in her lovely eyes. "I love to hunt. It gives me a thrill like nothin' else."

"Nothing?" Fargo said with a grin.

"Well, almost nothin'," Bobbie Joe allowed, and laughed. "But huntin' is in my blood. I started goin' after game as soon as I was big enough to hold a rifle, and I have been doin' it ever since."

"Squirrels and deer and bears don't shoot back."

Again she laughed. "True enough. But there is little challenge in goin' after them. Men on the run, on the other hand, use all sorts of tricks. Outsmartin' them is a thrill." She paused. "I seem to recollect that folks say you have hunted a few men in your time."

"When I had to," Fargo confirmed. "It can be a challenge, but I would never call it fun."

"What would you call fun, then?" Bobbie Joe asked, and when he roved his eyes from her hair to her toes, and grinned, she broke into the loudest laugh yet. "I should have known. That is all some men think about."

"Imagine that," Fargo said.

Old Charley kneed his mount over, spat a wad of tobacco juice, and showed his yellow teeth. "Morning, folks. I had me a nip of bug juice to get my blood flowing and am raring to go."

"You drink this early in the day?" Bobbie Joe asked.

"Hell, dearie, early or late it is all the same," Old Charley said. "And don't make me out to be booze blind. All I take is a nip from my flask now and again."

"What if we are gone so long, you run out?"

"I will shoot myself."

Deputy Gavin assumed the lead, saying over his shoulder to Fargo, "I will show you where the stage was struck. You pick up the trail and we will follow you."

It was not far. The tree the outlaws had felled across the road had since been rolled to one side. Fargo climbed down to scour the ground. So did Bobbie Joe and Old Charley.

There had not been any rain in a week and the ground was hard, but not so hard that an animal as heavy as a horse could avoid leaving tracks. And when there were four horses, and one was bearing double, the churned ground was as easy to read as the letters in a book.

Fargo swung onto his pinto and headed out. He had not covered twenty yards when Bobbie Joe caught up.

"Mind if I ride with you?"

"As easy as you are on the eyes, I would have to be loco to say no," Fargo replied.

"Am I going to have to beat you off with a club at night?" Bobbie Joe teasingly asked.

"I will wait until you are asleep before I crawl into your blankets," Fargo shot back. He found himself admiring how the breeze stirred her hair, and had to force himself to concentrate on the tracks and only the tracks.

Bobbie Joe had sharp eyes. "Is somethin' wrong?"

"You are a powerful distraction."

"That's not my fault," she returned. "I can't help it if I was born with a body men would give anything to touch."

"Humble, too," Fargo said.

"I am only sayin' how things are. If I am wrong, correct me."

"You are not wrong," Fargo confessed. "As for your body, so long as you keep your clothes on, I should be able to keep my mind on what I am supposed to be doing."

"Then you are safe. I generally only ride around naked on Sundays and today isn't Sunday."

After that, hardly anyone spoke. The tracks pointed south toward forested hills and distant mountains. The entire southwest corner of Missouri was the least inhabited region in the state. There were few homesteads and those few they soon passed. Ahead lay mile after mile of rugged wilderness, a natural haven for lawbreakers.

Noon came, and they were miles into the hills. Deputy Gavin hollered for Fargo to halt so they could rest the horses.

Kleb arched his back and complained that he hurt all over from so much riding. "I am not used to this. I am not used to this at all."

"Wait until tomorrow," Foley said. "You will feel worse."

"That wasn't a nice thing to say," Kleb told the big freighter. "Why can't you ever say anything nice? You are not the only one who has ever lost a loved one, you know."

Foley's jaw muscles twitched. "Mention my family again and I will snap your scrawny neck."

"Enough of that," Deputy Gavin intervened.

Lynch Spicer was sitting on a log, sipping from his canteen. "Hey, sweet thing," he called out to Bobbie Joe, and patted the log. "Why don't you come over and sit by me so we can get better acquainted."

"Why don't I jump off a cliff while I am at it?" was her retort.

"What is wrong with me?" Lynch demanded. "I am

the son of a judge. I have money. And all the girls say I am easy on the eyes."

"Stick with girls, boy," Bobbie Joe said. "Me, I am a woman, and I happen to prefer men."

Old Charley spat tobacco juice, then cackled. "A right friendly bunch we have here."

Fargo did not see the humor. A posse that did not get along, a posse that was frayed at the edges, was more apt to be torn apart by the hardships it encountered.

Deputy Gavin was having similar thoughts because he walked over and remarked so only Fargo heard, "We are barely under way and already there is too much squabbling. I can see I am going to have to keep a tight rein on these misfits."

"Send Foley and Lynch and Kleb back," Fargo suggested. "It will still be four against four."

"I would rather have an edge in numbers. The extra guns might make the difference." The deputy regarded the pockmarked soil. "At least the trail is easy to follow."

"Let's hope it stays that way."

It didn't.

A few miles on, they came to a rocky slope. The prints disappeared. Fargo assumed the outlaws had climbed to the top and gone on from there but when he reached the crest, the ground was undisturbed. He had to go back down and rove in a wide circle until he discovered where Terrell and company had reined to the southwest. It cost them a half hour.

"They can't give us the slip that easily," Bobbie Joe commented.

By late afternoon they were deep in the heart of the untamed wilds. The lush woodland teemed with animal life. More times than Fargo cared to count he spooked deer that bounded off with their tails raised in alarm. Lesser creatures were everywhere. Once he spotted, far off, a large black shape that might be a bear. They would not perish for lack of meat.

It was about four o'clock when Fargo came to a clearing and abruptly drew rein. "Damn," he said.

"Oh, hell," Bobbie Joe breathed.

The others came up behind them, and Deputy Gavin asked, "Why have you stopped? It is still early yet."

Fargo pointed. "See for yourself."

It was a dress. Once it had been a pretty dress with a floral print, now it was smudged and stained and torn in so many places, it was practically in tatters.

"Dear Lord!" Deputy Gavin exclaimed. "That fits the description of the dress Lucille Sparks was wearing."

Bobbie Joe reined her dun over to a mound of charred embers. "This is where they spent the night. One or all of them must have had their way with her."

"The poor woman," Old Charley said.

Dismounting, Deputy Gavin picked up what was left of the garment and examined it. "I can't find any blood. But I want everyone to search for her body, just in case."

They did not find one, though they spent over an hour at it, Kleb complaining the whole time that his back was hurting and his legs were hurting and even his feet were paining him.

Foley had taken all the grumbling he could. "You are worse than a woman."

"Here now," Bobbie Joe said. "You don't hear me gripin', do you?"

Kleb was flexing his legs and wincing. "I can't help it if I don't do as much riding as the rest of you. I haven't been on a horse in so long, I forget the last time. It's no wonder I am stiff and sore."

"Enough about your pains," Deputy Gavin said. "In two to three days you won't feel a thing."

"It will take that long for us to catch them?" Kleb asked, not sounding pleased.

"Longer, would be my guess," Gavin said. "But we are not giving up this side of the grave. Mad Dog Terrell's days of robbing and killing and taking women hostage are about over."

"He didn't take her as a hostage," Old Charley commented. "He took her because he wanted her. That dress proves it."

They pushed on. The deputy told Fargo to keep going

until it was too dark to see the tracks. By then they were on a high bench dotted with stands of trees. It was too open for Fargo's liking but Gavin called a halt for the night.

Indicating a cluster of trees close by, Fargo mentioned, "There would be better."

"Why?"

"Less chance of them spotting our fire. They are bound to be watching their back trail." Fargo well knew how a campfire could be seen for miles in the dark of night.

"I doubt that it makes much difference," Deputy Gavin responded. "They are bound to be expecting someone to come after them. But we will do what you want."

Fargo kindled the fire himself, and kept it small. He put coffee on to brew, leaned back against his saddle, and let himself relax for the first time that day.

Kleb was watching him from across the fire. "Are you just going to sit there? The deputy said we are to live off the land. Shouldn't you be off hunting?"

"It is too late in the day to hunt," Gavin answered before Fargo could. "Tomorrow he will. Tonight we will have to go without."

"Wonderful," Kleb muttered.

Old Charley had spread his blanket and opened a saddlebag. Taking out a packet of jerky, he tossed a piece to the townsman. "Here, you infant. I dried and salted the venison myself."

"I don't much like deer meat," Kleb said, his face scrunched in distaste.

"Then go hungry, you damned nuisance."

Deputy Gavin cleared his throat. "We must work harder to get along or this will turn into an ordeal."

"It already is," Kleb said, looking fit to cry. "Why you chose me for your posse, I will never know."

"You were handy, the same as the rest, and I did not have a lot of time to spare looking for someone better suited," Deputy Gavin justified his decision. "But don't worry. The next time I need to gather a posse, you are the last person I will ask."

"Thank God," Kleb said.

Fargo was waiting for steam to rise out of the coffee-pot. He was tired of the bickering, and it had been only one day. If things went on as they were, in a week they would be at each other's throats.

"You are awful quiet," Bobbie Joe commented. She had her blankets near his, and was on her back with her saddle for a pillow. The firelight playing over her enticing body and smooth complexion made her that much more lovely.

"I am not part chipmunk like some I could mention," Fargo said without thinking, and received a scowl from Kleb.

Lynch Spicer was on his knees, arranging his blankets. Smiling at Bobbie Joe, he crooked a finger. "Why don't you join me, pretty thing? We can keep each other warm."

"Why don't you stick your pistol in your mouth and save me the bother?" Bobbie Joe rejoined.

Foley chuckled, Kleb smirked, and Lynch Spicer colored with anger. "You are downright uppity for hill trash."

"Why, you miserable peckerwood." Bobbie Joe started to come up out of her blankets but Deputy Gavin motioned her back down.

"Enough! I won't say this again. Unless you have something pleasant to say, and this applies to all of you, keep your mouths shut."

Old Charley bit off some jerky and merrily chomped. "That's what I like about this world. It is swimming in brotherly love."

"What I said applies to you, too," Deputy Gavin said. "You will get along whether you want to or not."

Fargo toyed with the notion of sneaking off in the middle of the night and pushing on alone. With a little luck, he could end it that much sooner and be on his way west. Then the coffeepot burped, and he extended an arm to slide it a little closer to the fire.

That was when the night exploded with gunfire.

8

At the first shot Kleb cried out and nearly pitched into the fire, falling so close to it that his arm was licked by flames.

Bedlam erupted. Nearly everyone yelled and either froze in astonishment or bolted for cover.

A second shot kicked up dirt near Deputy Gavin.

"Away from the fire!" Fargo hollered while scrambling backward out of the light. The instant the dark enveloped him, he pushed into a crouch and drew his Colt.

A third shot cracked from out of the night but everyone had scattered except Kleb, who lay sprawled motionless.

This time Fargo saw the muzzle flash, and fired. It would be luck more than anything if he brought the bushwhacker down, but he wanted to buy precious seconds for the others to reach safety. He moved after he shot, darting to the left toward a stand of trees. He was almost to them when a figure reared in front of him. Instinctively, he leveled the Colt.

"Don't shoot! It's me!" Lynch Spicer squeaked. The whites of his eyes were showing. He had his revolver out and was waving it about as if he were swatting flies. "What do we do? Where did the others get to?"

"Quiet!" Fargo snapped, and flattened to listen and probe the night. He began reloading, the darkness forcing him to do it by touch alone.

Lynch dropped next to him, whispering, "Did you see what happened to Kleb? I was looking right at him. It was horrible, just horrible. I've never seen anyone killed before."

"You will be next if you don't shut up," Fargo warned, but he might as well have saved his breath.

"I can't believe they shot him like that. No warning, no nothing. What kind of men are we dealing with?"

"*Bad* men," Fargo answered. "Men who kill for the hell of it. Men who rob and rape and do as they please." He thought he saw movement off to the left. "You knew all that when we rode out of Springfield."

Lynch was staring at the prone form by the fire. "Knowing it and actually seeing somebody killed are two different things." His face had become as pale as a sheet. "I don't know if I can do this. Honest to God I don't."

"Take it up with Gavin later. Right now you need to stay calm and not let out a peep."

Spicer fell quiet.

Fargo strained his ears but all he heard was the rustle of the breeze in the trees overhead. The killer had not fired again, so either by some miracle his own shot had scored or the man had lit a shuck.

Time crawled on a snail's belly. Fargo was about to rise and prowl in search of the shooter when a female voice was raised in the direction the shots came from.

"It is all right! He is gone!"

Fargo rose and made for the fire. Old Charley appeared, then Foley. Despite Bobbie Joe's yell, they moved as if walking on eggshells, their revolvers in their hands.

Careful not to step in the scarlet pool, Fargo rolled Kleb over. The slug had caught the clerk in the throat. Some of his blood had spread into the fire and the flames were giving off a loud hiss. A pungent odor filled the air.

"I told you it was horrible," Lynch Spicer said.

Old Charley spat tobacco. "At least he went quick. I doubt he knew what hit him."

"You almost make it sound like a good way to die," Lynch complained.

"Hell, boy," Old Charley replied. "Good or bad has nothing to do with it. Dead is dead."

Bobbie Joe Jentry materialized out of the darkness. To Fargo she said, "I think you scared him off. I heard him run away and then the sound of hooves."

Fargo selected the unlit end of a burning brand and raised it aloft. "We will have a look."

Unnoticed, Deputy Gavin had been silently staring at the body. Now he stepped forward, saying, "I will tend to the burying."

"Shouldn't we take him back to Springfield and plant him proper?" Lynch Spicer asked. "It doesn't seem right to dig a hole in the middle of nowhere and drop him in it."

"He doesn't have any family that I know of," Gavin said, "and I can't spare anyone to tote him back." He bent and gripped Kleb's ankles. "Someone give me a hand."

Both Old Charley and Foley moved to help. Lynch Spicer stared, a fine sheen of sweat glistening on his skin.

Fargo shucked his Henry from his saddle scabbard, then gestured at Bobbie Joe and fell into step beside her. She did not say anything until they were out of earshot of the others.

"That Spicer boy is startin' to worry me. He is as high-strung as a cat in a room full of rockin' chairs. It wouldn't surprise me any if he proves worthless if we have to swap lead with Mad Dog's bunch."

"Like you said earlier, he is a boy in a man's clothes."

"Are you defendin' him?"

"No," Fargo replied. "But I don't hold it against him that he is not used to blood and killing. He has been coddled all his life."

"The poor infant."

"That is harsh," Fargo said.

"I have no use for city folk," Bobbie Joe said in contempt. "Them and their prissy ways."

"Not everyone likes the backwoods."

"It is more than that. Take them out of the city and they are helpless. Not one in a hundred can fend for himself. Only a few know how to hunt. Most can't

58

butcher an animal or skin it or find water or even tell north from south and east from west."

Fargo did not say anything. She had a point, to a point.

"If a law were passed tomorrow that everyone had to make their own clothes, most city folk would have to traipse around naked. Left alone out here, they would starve. If that isn't worthless, I don't know what is."

"City folk made that rifle you are holding and that revolver of yours," Fargo noted. "Your knife, that belt with its brass buckle, and those boots of yours, too. You didn't make any of them yourself."

"I am not sayin' there aren't some things city folk are good for," Bobbie Joe said. "I am sayin' they are infants, like the judge's boy. He should be sent back before he gets himself killed."

She had another point. "I will talk to Gavin when we get back to camp," Fargo said.

"You do that. I doubt he would listen to me, me bein' a lowly female and all."

"Do you sharpen that tongue of yours every morning or were you born with a dagger in your mouth?"

Bobbie Joe chuckled in delight. "I say my piece. If that is too sharp-tongued for some, they can plug their ears with wax." She stopped and looked about. "This is about where I heard him."

Several oaks loomed. Evidently the rifleman had crouched behind one of them. Fargo held the torch out and made a thorough sweep but his hopes were dashed. "No blood."

"It must be the same jasper you told me took a shot at you last night," Bobbie Joe speculated. "One of Mad Dog's men, I reckon."

"Could be," Fargo allowed, although he was at a loss as to why the man tried to kill him back at Dawson's Corners. "Maybe it was Mad Dog himself."

"Not him. He's not the sort to shoot from ambush. He likes to walk right up to you and look you in the eyes when he kills you. It is the one good trait he has."

"You call that good?"

"Compared to his other traits, yes. He is not like you and me. He does not put any value at all on human life. He thinks we are no better than bugs, to be squashed when and where he wants. He killed his first man when he was ten. The owner of a general store, who wouldn't let him have a foldin' knife he had taken a shine to. So Mad Dog opened that knife and stabbed the man in the gut. Then as the man lay on the floor screamin', Mad Dog walked out, laughin', with the knife."

"Suddenly you know a whole hell of a lot about Mad Dog Terrell and his past."

"I told you. My family ran into him and his wild bunch once. We talked some around the campfire that night. I'm naturally the curious sort, so I asked him a lot of questions I probably shouldn't have. But damn me if he didn't answer them like a true gentleman."

"What else did he say that I should know?"

Bobbie Joe shrugged. "Mostly it was personal stuff. About his pa, who drank himself to death when Mad Dog was six. About his ma, who beat him a lot until he got old enough to beat her back. About a cousin of his he loved, who refused to have anything to do with him."

Fargo could see a man like Terrell, who spent most of his time on the run and did not get to spend much time with women, opening up to someone as pretty as Bobbie Joe. But something troubled him. "I can't get over that he didn't try to harm you or your family."

"We didn't give him cause to, and we didn't have money or valuables of any kind." Bobbie Joe paused. "Plus, like I told you, there were about twenty of us and only the four of them, and we all had guns."

"Why didn't you disarm Mad Dog and turn him over to the law?"

Bobbie Joe stared at him in mild shock. "Me and mine never go to the law. If someone wrongs us, we do as the Bible says. An eye for an eye, a tooth for a tooth."

Again, Fargo thought he understood. Most hill clans wanted nothing to do with the outside world.

"Mad Dog behaved himself that night," Bobbie Joe had gone on. "He gave us no cause to think ill of him, even if we were inclined to hand him over, which we weren't."

Fargo turned. His torch was near to going out, and he began to retrace their steps, saying, "What about the men who ride with him? What can you tell me about them?"

"Mattox is big and dumb. Bigger even than Foley and likely twice as strong. He does what Mad Dog wants him to do, no questions asked. DePue is a Cajun or some such and fancies himself a treat for the ladies, but he is too oily for my taste. Yoas is a breed. I am not sure of the exact mix, but he is snake mean and gets a thrill out of snuffin' life. You mentioned a dagger a while ago. Yoas carries one. Double-edged, with a silver hilt. He is a wizard with it. We watched him toss and twirl it like you would not believe. He can use it with either hand, the one as good as the other. They have a word for that but I'll be hanged if I can ever remember what the word is."

Fargo had to think some himself. "Ambidextrous."

"That's the one," Bobbie Joe said with a nod. "Who comes up with stupid words like that? Words nobody can hardly half say or recollect? I bet it's some Easterner sittin' in one of those soft easy chairs drinkin' his brandy, with nothin' better to do."

A figure abruptly appeared and Fargo raised his Henry. Enough light was cast by the few flames on his torch that in another step he recognized who it was and what he was doing.

"It must be hard to dig with that broken tree branch," Bobbie Joe said to Deputy Gavin.

The lawman stopped and mopped at his brow with a sleeve. Near him lay the body, wrapped in a blanket. "We didn't bring a shovel."

"No one is helping you?" Fargo asked.

"It is mine to do. I am the leader of the posse." Gavin grunted as he jabbed the branch into the earth and pried out a clod.

Bobbie Joe remarked, "At that rate it will take you half the night."

"It serves me right for not posting a sentry," Deputy Gavin said. "If I had, maybe Kleb would still be alive."

"The killer was too far off," Fargo mentioned. "A sentry would not have spotted him."

"Maybe a sentry would have heard something. A twig snap. A hoofbeat. Anything. Sounds we didn't hear because we were all talking."

"Don't be so hard on yourself," Bobbie Joe advised. "We all make mistakes."

"Mine cost a man who did not want to be here his life," the deputy said as he used the branch again. "If I did not feel bad about it, it would make me as coldhearted as Mad Dog Terrell."

"Now see," Bobbie Joe said. "Folks just naturally jump to conclusions about him. He might surprise you."

Gavin did not respond. He was jabbing with a fury. Fargo nudged Bobbie Joe and they walked on. The torch finally went out but Fargo held on to it, intending to drop the brand in the fire. They had only a short way to go when Bobbie Joe, who had been deep in thought, made a comment that suggested she was thinking aloud.

"Maybe I did wrong comin' on this hunt."

"Speaking for myself, I am glad you did," Fargo said, and grinned. "You are a lot easier on the eyes than the others."

Bobbie Joe gave a slight start, and smiled. "You can't help yourself, can you, when it comes to the ladies?"

"No, but I have a good excuse."

"Besides bein' male?"

"A curse was placed on me by a gypsy woman when I was sixteen. She said I was doomed to go through life chasing every pretty woman I saw, and it has turned out true," Fargo embellished.

Bobbie Joe burst out laughing but her mirth died in her throat as they came to the campfire and beheld Old Charley lying in a twisted heap on the ground with blood trickling from a corner of his mouth. Fargo was about to squat and see if the old frontiersman was still alive when

Lynch Spicer stepped out of the dark with his Remington revolver leveled.

"What the hell?" Bobbie Joe exclaimed.

"I wish you hadn't come back," Lynch said regretfully. Then he cocked the revolver.

9

Bobbie Joe Jentry did not do as many women would. She did not freeze in fear, or shriek, or indulge in emotional hysterics. She calmly stood there and asked the question Fargo was about to ask. "What in God's name have you done, boy?"

"Don't call me that," Lynch Spicer said. He gestured at the prone figure bleeding by the fire. "I told that old coot I was leaving and he tried to stop me. So I gave him a wallop on the noggin with this." Lynch wagged the Remington.

"You better hope he comes to," Fargo said.

"He shouldn't have interfered!" Lynch said shrilly. "All I want is to go home!"

"Back to your important papa and your sweet little lady friends and actin' as if you are somebody when you are not," Bobbie Joe said.

Lynch angrily snapped, "What does backwoods trash like you know about anything?"

"I know enough not to go around wallopin' folks without more cause than you had."

"Where is Foley?" Fargo asked.

"He went off to collect more firewood," Lynch answered. "With him and the deputy gone, I saw my chance and I took it." He stared to back away. "Now I am leaving, and I don't want either of you to try and stop me. I will shoot if I have to. I swear I will shoot."

"No more brains than a turnip," Bobbie Joe said.

Fargo was holding the charred brand next to his leg.

64

It was about two feet long and as thick as his forearm. Suddenly pointing with his other hand into the dark behind Spicer, he exclaimed, "Isn't that Foley there?"

Lynch Spicer reacted without thinking and turned to see for himself.

Quick as thought, Fargo threw the brand. It caught the younger man on the side of the head, knocking his hat off. Lynch let out a yelp and spun but Fargo was already on him, the Colt out, and gave him a taste of the same treatment he had given Old Charley. With a loud cry the younger man folded at the knees.

"That was mighty slick," Bobbie Joe complimented him.

Fargo plucked the Remington from Lynch's limp fingers and wedged it under his own belt.

"He doesn't know it, but you saved him from bein' shot," Bobbie Joe said. "I wasn't about to let him go ridin' off."

"You are as bloodthirsty as Mad Dog Terrell," Fargo joked as he rolled Lynch onto his back and frisked him for other weapons. There were none.

Boots drummed, and out of the night rushed Deputy Gavin. "What is all the ruckus about?" he asked, and stopped short when he saw the two forms on the ground. "Tell me they are not dead."

"They're not," Bobbie Joe confirmed. "But they will both have god-awful headaches when they come around."

Fargo explained the situation as he opened his canteen and poured some water into his tin cup. Just enough that when he upended the cup over Old Charley's face, the frontiersman sputtered and coughed and sat up as riled as an agitated bear.

"Where is he? Where is that no-account sprout? I will learn him to pound on his elders!"

"Simmer down," Fargo said, and nodded at where Lynch lay. "I did you the favor."

Deputy Gavin helped Old Charley to stand. "I appreciate you trying to stop him but maybe it would have been better if you let him go."

"That is a fine note after he damn near split my skull

for me doing your job," Old Charley grumbled. "As a posse we are next to pitiful."

Gavin's lips pinched together. "I deserve that. I accept the blame for not keeping an eye on him."

"Is it me, sonny," Old Charley said, "or are you fond of toting the world on your shoulders? None of us are perfect. You ought to keep that in mind when you go blaming yourself for everything under the sun."

Bobbie Joe broke in, asking, "What are we goin' to do about the judge's son? I say we string him up by his thumbs and leave him hangin' until we are done with Mad Dog."

Deputy Gavin stepped to Lynch and shook him, eliciting a low groan but nothing else.

Fargo refilled his cup with steaming hot coffee and sank down cross-legged with his back to the fire. Old Charley was exactly right. They *were* doing pitiful, and if things did not change a lot worse was bound to happen.

"I should not have picked Lynch for the posse," Deputy Gavin remarked as he raised Spicer into a sitting position.

Old Charley spat out the wad of tobacco in his mouth, and swore. "You are a weak sister, law dog. You truly are."

"I agree," Bobbie Joe chimed in.

Fargo had listened to enough. "Ease off him," he said. The last thing they needed was for the deputy to doubt himself even worse than he already did. He turned to Gavin. "You did what you thought best. The thing now is to take charge and not make any mistakes."

Deputy Gavin nodded. "I will start with Lynch." From under his vest he produced handcuffs and proceeded to snap them onto Spicer's wrists.

"Shouldn't you save them for Mad Dog and his killers?" Old Charley asked.

"I have another set in my saddlebags if I need them," Gavin said.

"That is not what I meant."

The deputy shook Lynch Spicer again, harder than before.

This time Lynch's eyelids fluttered and he mumbled and then opened his eyes and looked around in confusion. His confusion grew when he moved his arms and discovered the cuffs. "What are these for?"

"I am placing you under arrest for assaulting Old Charley," Deputy Gavin announced.

"You can't do this!" Lynch bleated, panic in his tone. "I am helpless with these on."

"You should have thought of that before you hit him," Gavin said. "I am afraid I must make an example of you."

"Arrest me if you have to when we get back to Springfield," Lynch said. "But not here. Not now."

"You have brought it on yourself." Rising, Deputy Gavin slid his hand under Spicer's arm and hauled him nearer to the fire. "Have a seat. The others will keep an eye on you while I go finish digging Kleb's grave."

Lynch was staring at the handcuffs in mixed outrage and horror. "Wait until my father hears of this! Wait until I tell him how I have been treated! You won't be wearing that badge much longer, I promise you!"

Ignoring him, Gavin walked off.

"I mean it!" Lynch screeched after him. "My father will see to it that you are stripped of that tin star and run out of Springfield! No one does this to me! No one!"

Old Charley sighed. "Give your tonsils a rest, boy. He is not listening and you are making the headache you gave me worse."

"To hell with you, too!" Lynch snarled. "You wretched old buzzard, getting me into this fix."

"Me?" Old Charley responded. "Who hit who?"

Lynch was not given the chance to answer. Bobbie Joe Jentry's left hand moved and her knife glinted in the firelight. Before anyone could stop her, she pressed the tip to his throat.

"I have had my fill of you, boy, of your whinin' and bellyachin'. Not another peep, you hear, or I will cut you."

"Bitch," Lynch said, but he subsided and glumly placed his elbows on his legs and his chin in his hands.

"That's better," Bobbie Joe said, replacing her knife in its sheath.

"I hate you. I hate all of you."

About then Foley came out of the woods, his big arms burdened with enough firewood to last a week. He set the wood down, scanned their faces, and asked, "What have I missed?"

By midnight the only one awake was Fargo. He had agreed to take the first watch. Except for the snoring of Foley and Old Charley, the night was quiet. The horses were dozing. The fire had dwindled to a few tiny flames. In the inky canopy above sparkled a multitude of stars. Fargo noted the position of the Big Dipper. He was supposed to wake Bobbie Joe soon so she could take over.

His pinto chose that moment to raise its head and prick its ears to the southwest.

Instantly alert, Fargo rose into a crouch. He was about five yards from the others, where he was less apt to be spotted by nocturnal prowlers. Wedging the Henry's stock to his shoulder, he watched the Ovaro. When it nickered and stamped a front hoof, he peered in the same direction the horse was staring, peered until his eyes were fit to burst from their sockets, but he saw nothing to account for the Ovaro's behavior.

Then something moved off in the murk, something low to the ground, flowing swiftly toward the sleepers.

Fargo's first thought was that the rifleman had returned, but as the shape came closer he saw that it was an animal, a predator, he suspected, drawn by their scent or the scent of their horses. The thing stopped, and he could not quite make out what it was. If he fired, he might just wound it, and wounded meat eaters were known to go berserk with fury.

A cramp in his leg caused Fargo to shift ever so slightly, yet that was enough. Instantly, the creature swung toward him. Reflected in the faint glow of the fire were a pair of slanted eyes. Blazing yellow, they told Fargo what he was up against: a cougar.

Normally the big cats left humans alone. Normally, but not always. A Crow warrior Fargo knew had been scarred for life when a mountain lion jumped him. The Crow had been eight years old at the time, picking berries with his mother and sisters, and the cougar leaped on his back and bore him down. His mother's scream saved him. It brought the father on the run, and he happened to have his bow with him. The father loosed a barbed shaft that pierced the cat's heart but not before the cougar had raked the right side of the boy's face with its razor claws, missing the boy's eye but ripping so deep that ever after the Crow bore the marks.

A growl ended Fargo's reverie. The cougar was slinking toward him, its long tail twitching, about to attack. He sighted between its eyes, thankful for the firelight that enabled him to align the sights.

The cougar stopped. Its tail went rigid.

Fargo braced himself.

At that moment Bobbie Joe Jentry sat up, yawned, gazed sleepily about her and asked, "Fargo? Isn't it time for me to spell you?"

Fargo shot to his feet. He expected the cougar to charge her. But it did no such thing; instead, it hissed, whirled, and raced off into the forest. He grinned grimly. Cougars, like bears and wolves, shared a trait in common. They were unpredictable.

Bobbie Joe said his name again. Fargo went over, the Henry in the crook of his elbow. "Do you scare off grizzlies, too?"

"How is that?"

Fargo told her about the cat. "Keep an eye out in case it comes back. We can't afford to lose any of the horses."

"We can afford to lose one," Bobbie Joe said with a grin. "Kleb won't be needin' his."

Fargo had forgotten about the clerk. The man meant nothing to him personally, but the cold manner in which she joked about his death was a trifle surprising. "No, I reckon he won't."

Sleep came easily. Fargo was bone tired. He slept with the Henry at his side and his Colt in his hand on his chest under his blanket. His dreams were fitful, images of phantom assassins who walked on two legs but had the heads of mountain lions. He would have sworn he had barely been asleep an hour when a hand on his shoulder roughly shaking him brought him back to the world of the living.

Dawn would soon break. Foley was kindling the fire. It had been Old Charley's turn to keep watch, and it was his hand on Fargo's shoulder. "Come with me, hoss. There is something you might want to see."

Sluggish as molasses, Fargo rose, holstered the Colt, and followed the seasoned frontiersman to a spot twenty yards from their camp. A gray tinge marked the eastern horizon but other than that the sky was ink black. "What is so important?" Fargo asked.

Old Charley extended an arm to the southwest. "I didn't notice it until a short while ago. If you don't see it right away, wait a bit."

Fargo looked and saw only the mantle of night. He did as Charley suggested, and when all he continued to see was an unbroken vista of pitch, he started to turn to ask exactly what Charley expected him to see. Then he saw it. Fleeting, lasting no more than two or three heartbeats, but there was no mistaking the pinpoint of light for anything other than what it was. "You have good eyes, old-timer."

"Mad Dog's campfire, you reckon?"

"Who else would it be?" Fargo rejoined. At that time of year few hunters penetrated this far into the wilds.

"How far do you make it?"

Fargo was attempting to gauge that very thing. Distances were deceiving at night. A campfire might seem to be close when actually it was miles away. This one, though, *was* miles away.

As it turned out, two miles, or thereabouts. The embers were still giving off wisps of smoke when they reined up in the hollow where the outlaws had camped. Fargo swung down and sought tracks. He was the first to notice a stick embedded in the ground next to a log that had been dragged close to the fire for the outlaws to sit on.

The end of the stick had been split and a folded piece of paper wedged fast.

Deputy Gavin had noticed it, too. "What is that there?"

Fargo removed the paper from the slit and unfolded it. In a barely legible scrawl was a message, short and to the point.

"What does it say?" Deputy Gavin prompted.

Fargo raised his voice so they all could hear. "Turn around and go back or the woman dies."

10

If Mad Dog Terrell's plan was to delay them, it worked.

Deputy Gavin took the paper from Fargo and read the note for himself. "Lucille Sparks is as good as dead no matter what we do. Mad Dog can't leave her alive, not when she can testify in court against him. Her only hope is for us to rescue her. We are pushing on."

"Not so fast, law dog," Foley said. "We should talk this over. It might be best for the Sparks girl if we do as they want."

"I agree," Lynch Spicer quickly said. "If our pushing on gets her killed, then what good have we done? We came all this way for nothing. Kleb lost his life for nothing. I say we do as they want and turn around and go back."

"What you want," Deputy Gavin informed him, "is of no consequence. You have no say in this. You gave it up when you attacked another posse member."

"You are dragging me along against my will, aren't you?" Lynch argued. "That gives me a say whether you like it or not."

Old Charley spat tobacco juice. "No one has asked my opinion but if they did I would tell them that Mad Dog has us over a barrel, and he knows it. He is out there somewhere laughing himself silly at our expense."

"Talk, talk, talk," Bobbie Joe Jentry criticized. "That is all this posse is good for. While we sit here jawin', that girl you all claim to be so concerned about might be bein' abused."

No one asked what she meant by abused. They did not have to.

Deputy Gavin looked at Fargo. "We have not heard from our scout yet. What is your considered opinion?"

Fargo chose his words carefully. "I agree with you that Mad Dog won't let her live. If we go back, she dies anyway. But if we push on, she might die that much sooner. He is bound to be watching us from a distance, him or one of his men, while the rest went on with Lucy." At that some of them began glancing all around and nervously fingering their weapons. "Stop that!" Fargo warned. "Let them think we don't suspect. We can use it against them."

"I am listening," Deputy Gavin said.

"I say we make camp. We will sit around the fire and talk. That will give whoever is watching the idea that we are talking it over."

"What then?" Bobbie Joe asked.

"One of us slips away and goes on alone," Fargo proposed. "One person has a better chance of sneaking up on them than all of us together."

"I take it that you mean for that person to be you?" Deputy Gavin asked.

Fargo nodded. He was the best qualified. "Unless you have a better idea."

Bobbie Joe objected. "But what if all of them are out there watchin' us, not just one? They are bound to notice when you slip away, and will be ready for you. One of us should go with you to watch your back."

"I will go with him," Deputy Gavin said.

"It can't be you," Bobbie Joe responded. "You have to watch over Spicer. Besides, it should be someone who can move through the woods as quietly as a mouse, and that would be me."

"I can be as quiet as you, girl," Old Charley said.

"Maybe you can," Bobbie Joe admitted. "But you mentioned once that you are not as spry as you used to be. Well, I am spry and then some." She grinned. "You stay and rest those old joints of yours."

Deputy Gavin looked at Fargo. "I leave the decision up to you. Who will it be? Old Charley or Bobbie Joe?"

Fargo pondered. The old scout or a backwoodswoman. In his estimation they were about equal except that, as Bobbie Joe had brought up, Old Charley was older. But he did not hold Charley's age against him. Maybe the old frontiersman was a shade slower than he used to be but his vast experience more than made up for it. Even so, Fargo said, "I pick Bobbie Joe."

Old Charley spat tobacco juice, this time in disgust. "Why her and not me?"

"I want you in reserve in case they get us," Fargo said. "Gavin will need someone he can depend on."

"And he can't depend on me?" Bobbie Joe asked, sounding as if her feelings were hurt.

"You are the one who volunteered," Fargo reminded her.

"It is settled, then," Deputy Gavin announced. "Foley, you make the fire. Take your time and put on a show for whoever is spying on us."

"Why am I always the one who does the fire?" the big freighter rumbled. "The rest of you should take turns."

"You will do it because I say to do it," Deputy Gavin said. "That I always pick you is neither here nor there."

"The hell you say," Foley complained, but he did as he was told.

Fargo contrived to have the Ovaro near the trees when he dismounted. He waited with the others while Foley gathered wood and watched with them as Foley nursed a flame to life. Then he sat with them for a while and pretended to listen while Gavin gave a short speech about how it was the civic duty of every citizen to oppose lawlessness.

Then, with a glance at Bobbie Joe, Fargo rose and walked into the woods. To an onlooker it might appear he had gone for more firewood or to heed nature's call. He whistled softly, and the Ovaro came to him as he had trained it to do.

Bobbie Joe lingered a few minutes. Then she, too, rose and entered the trees, leading her horse by the reins.

Fargo promptly mounted and gigged the pinto. Sticking to cover, he rode to the southwest.

Right behind him came Bobbie Joe.

They had gone a half mile when the ground steeply climbed. In a few hundred yards they came to the top of a ridge. Reining up, Fargo rose in the stirrups and scanned the woods. He did not spot anyone but he did see their camp, plain as could be. "If there is a watcher, he must be close," he whispered, and dismounted. "You wait here while I scout around."

"Nothin' doin'," Bobbie Joe replied. "I did not come along to nursemaid the horses."

Fargo removed his spurs and slipped them into his saddlebags. Together they crept along the ridge. He made no more noise than that cougar the night before. To her credit, neither did Bobbie Joe.

They had not gone far when Fargo stopped and stiffened. He had heard a hoof stamp. A tangle of briars blocked his view. He could not see over them so he went around, circling until he glimpsed black amid the green. It was a hat, a wide-brimmed black hat such as Indians favored, only this one was on the head of a short, stocky man whose features hinted at a mix of red and white and perhaps a little brown thrown in.

"Yoas," Bobbie Joe whispered.

The half-breed was leaning against a tree and gazing down at the camp in the hollow. Every now and then he rose onto his toes, although what benefit that did him, Fargo could not imagine.

Of the other outlaws, there was no sign.

"We will wait for him to move on," Fargo whispered.

"He won't be easy to shadow," Bobbie Joe responded. "He has the eyes of a hawk and the ears of a fox."

Yoas was also apparently in no hurry to catch up to his companions. A half hour went by. An hour.

"Maybe Mad Dog told him not to rejoin the outlaws until the posse leaves," Bobbie Joe ventured.

Fargo had been thinking the same thing.

Yoas abruptly proved them wrong by wheeling and wending purposefully among the boles. He did not go far. His horse was concealed among some pines.

Fargo did not linger to watch the killer ride off. Turning, he made haste for the pinto, Bobbie Joe at his side every stride of the way. They quickly mounted and headed southwest. Soon they spied the breed.

Fargo did not follow directly behind but instead paralleled the outlaw's course. Every now and again he glimpsed Yoas far off through the trees. His worry was that the breed might catch sight of them. To prevent that, he avoided open spaces as much as was possible.

Two hours went by. Bobbie Joe did not utter a word in all that time, until, clearing her throat, she quietly asked, "What will you do if he leads us to the rest?"

To Fargo it was a silly question. "What else? Get Lucille Sparks out in one piece."

"I doubt we can do it without killin' Mad Dog and his men."

Fargo considered that observation even sillier. "They are the scourge of Missouri. No one will miss them."

"What if we can get her away from them without killin' them?"

Twisting in the saddle, Fargo regarded the hill girl. "Are you leading up to something or talking to hear yourself talk?"

"I was just askin'," Bobbie Joe said defensively.

It puzzled him, but Fargo promptly forgot about it as he devoted his energies to shadowing Yoas. They were well into the mountains and pressing deeper, the land a virgin paradise of lush forest teeming with abundant wildlife. Ages past, all of Missouri had been like this. Now, much of it was cultivated farmland, with more space taken each year by settlements and towns and cities. Only here, in the southwest corner, was Missouri pretty much as it had been before the coming of the white man. Only here, in the maze of mountains, waterways, and caves, could badmen like Mad Dog Terrell find a haven from the long arm of the law.

Until now.

Fargo could count the number of times he had been deputized on one hand. It was not that he did not believe in law and order. Without law, the frontier would be overrun by its wilder elements. As it was, cutthroats and renegades were as thick as fleas on a hound dog. Law and order were necessary, provided they were not taken too far.

Fargo had been to places back east where a man couldn't spit without being arrested. Places where the boardwalks were rolled up at sundown. Places where saloons and taverns were banned, gambling was considered a vile vice, and ladies were required to act accordingly in every sense of the word. He never could understand why people were content to live that way. To him, whiskey and women and cards were the spice that made civilization bearable. Without them, town and city life was a dull drudge. People got up, they went to work, they came home, they went to bed. That was it. Day in and day out, year in and year out. Their entire world might consist of fifty square miles of real estate, if that.

Such a life was not for him. Fargo hated to be hemmed in as much as he hated to be shackled by so-called virtue. He liked to drink when he wanted and play poker when he wanted and treat himself to a willing gal when she wanted. He liked to roam, to wander, to explore, to see each and every day a part of the world he had never seen before.

Wisps of gray rose in the distance. Smoke, rising from a campfire.

Fargo glimpsed Yoas once more, high up on a thinly timbered spine that separated the slope they were climbing from whatever lay on the other side.

"It won't be long now," Bobbie Joe whispered. She did not sound happy about it.

"No, it won't," Fargo agreed.

From the spine they looked down on a hidden valley nestled amid stark mountains and watered by a meandering stream. In the very center of the valley, approximately a half mile off, stood a solitary cabin. From its stone chimney curled the smoke they had seen. Attached to the cabin was a corral with more than a half dozen horses.

"Will you look at that," Bobbie Joe said. "As snug as can be, and no one knows about it except them."

"And us," Fargo amended. "I want you to ride back and fetch the deputy and the others."

"No."

Fargo wasn't sure he had heard her right. "No?"

"The deputy did not put you in charge of me," Bobbie Joe said. "I am free to do as I please, and it pleases me to sneak on down there and give Mad Dog the surprise of his life."

"One of us needs to get the rest of the posse," Fargo insisted.

"Don't let me hold you up."

Fargo looked at her. "Why are you being so pigheaded?"

"Don't beat around the bush," Bobbie Joe smirked. "Come right out with what is on your mind."

"I am serious." Until this moment, she had struck Fargo as fairly levelheaded.

"I am not your errand girl. I intend to go down there and find the Sparks woman. You are welcome to tag along or you can go after the deputy or sit here and twiddle your thumbs for all I care." So saying, Bobbie Joe clucked to her dun and rode past him.

Fargo simmered inside. She had been acting contrary all morning, and now this. Short of knocking her over the head and tying her up, he was forced to jab his heels against the Ovaro and follow her.

Heavy timber screened them from scrutiny. At the bottom they drew rein. Except for the trees that fringed the stream, the valley floor was open grassland.

"We can't get anywhere near their hideout without bein' spotted," Bobbie Joe remarked. "Maybe we should wait until dark."

It was Fargo's turn to say, "No. The sooner we get Lucille out of there, the better off she will be."

"Whatever you want," Bobbie Joe said with more than a touch of amusement.

They circled to where the stream entered the woods. Staying on the opposite side from the cabin, they picked their way among the cottonwoods and willows and oaks. Fargo had the Henry across his saddle. The only window he saw was covered by burlap. Presently they came abreast of the cabin, and he drew rein. "We will leave the horses here, cross the stream on foot, and crawl the rest of the way," he proposed.

"I have a better idea."

"Why am I not surprised?" Fargo said, and shifted in his saddle. "Let me hear—" He stopped when he saw she was pointing her rifle at him.

"My idea is for you to do exactly as I tell you. At this range I can't miss."

11

"Have you gone loco?" Fargo asked. He made no attempt to raise his rifle or go for his Colt.

Bobbie Joe Jentry frowned. "I don't particularly want to hurt you but I will if you force me. If you think I won't shoot because I am a woman, you are mistaken. I have shot folks before, and I am no bluff. I have heard you are slick on the draw but if you think you can get off a shot before I do, you are mistaken."

Fargo tried another tack. "What is this about?"

"You will find out in a bit. In the meantime, shove your rifle into your saddle scabbard but do it slow."

Fargo complied. He had no doubt she would do as she said. There was a moment, just before he slid the rifle in, when he considered swinging it like a club and trying to knock her rifle from her hands. But the steely gleam in her otherwise lovely eyes warned him he had better not.

"Thank you," Bobbie Joe said. "Now head straight for the cabin, and no shenanigans."

"They might shoot us off our horses before we get there," Fargo felt compelled to mention.

Bobbie Joe tittered. "You, maybe, but I doubt they will shoot me. Mad Dog would not let them."

On that enigmatic note, Fargo kneed the pinto across the stream and through the trees on the other side. As he emerged into the open, the sun struck him full in the face. He blinked against the glare and focused on the cabin, on the burlap flap over the window and on the door.

"You could at least explain," he tried again without turning his head.

"Hush. Another minute or two and it will all be clear."

The burlap flap moved and a face appeared. It was there and it was gone. Not five seconds later the front door opened wide and out came three of the outlaws.

The last to emerge was the breed, Yoas. The other two were as different as night from day. One was huge, even larger than Foley, with fists the size of mallets and great thick shoulders worthy of a bull. His beard was a riot of hair that had never been brushed, combed or trimmed. The other man, by contrast, was almost as short as Yoas and so thin and pale as to appear fragile. His mustache was no thicker than string. Where the huge hulk wore grimy homespun, the thin one wore the kind of clothes favored by men who lived in bayou country.

Based on what he had been told, Fargo reckoned that the huge one was Mattox and the other must be DePue, which proved to be the case.

"*Mon Dieu!* What have we here? To what do we owe the *honneur* of your visit, mademoiselle?"

"I am lookin' for Mad Dog," Bobbie Joe said. "I have somethin' important to tell him."

"And a gift, too, I see, *ma chère*," DePue said, grinning. "Who might this fine fellow with you be, *mon amie*?"

Bobbie Joe told him, adding, "And how many times must I tell you not to call me your sweetheart?"

DePue put a hand to his chest as if in pain. "Ah, mademoiselle, I am stricken. To have one so fair accord me such little notice—it is a humiliation I can not bear."

"Still as full of it as ever," Bobbie Joe said.

Mattox let out with a great roar of a laugh and slapped his tree trunk of a thigh. "That is what I like about you, girl! You always put that uppity Creole in his place."

DePue let out with an exaggerated sigh. "Will you never get it right, you mountain of muscle? I am Cajun, not Creole. *Comprenez-vous?*"

Mattox shrugged his enormous shoulders. "Cajun. Creole. They are all the same to me."

"Not to me," DePue said. "I take pride in my heritage."

"You are a runt who talks funny," Mattox said. "What is there to be proud about?"

DePue colored and moved his jacket aside to reveal a Smith & Wesson revolver, worn butt forward. "If Mad Dog did not insist I keep you alive, I would use you for target practice."

Mattox laughed some more. "You are welcome to try, puny man. But even if you empty your six-gun into me, I will still reach you and break your scrawny Cajun neck."

"Aha!" DePue exclaimed, clapping his hands in mock delight. "You can get it right when you try! You are not the utter imbecile you make yourself out to be."

At that juncture Yoas stepped past them, growling. "That's enough, senor, out of you and him both." He glared at Fargo, then gave Bobbie Joe a quizzical look. "How did you find us, senorita? Mad Dog never brought you here that I know of."

"We followed you."

Mattox's bushy eyebrows practically met over his bulbous nose. "You don't say, missy? Awful sloppy of you, breed."

Whirling, Yoas hovered his hand over his holster. "I have told you before, gringo. Do not call me that. Do not *ever* call me that."

"I will call you what I damn well please," Mattox informed him. "And if you don't like it, you are as welcome as the Frenchman to do something about it."

Fargo hoped they would come to blows, or worse. He was ever so slowly inching his hand toward his Colt. If they kept it up a little longer, they were in for an unwelcome shock.

Behind him, a gun hammer clicked. "No, you don't," Bobbie Joe said. "You have behaved so far. Keep on behaving and I will keep you alive."

Yoas had also heard the click. Turning, he stepped to the pinto and relieved Fargo of the Colt and the Henry, saying as he did, "We are sloppy. We should have disarmed you first thing."

Mattox came over, hooked his gigantic hands under Fargo's arms, and swung Fargo to the ground as easily as Fargo might swing a feather. "Why don't you join us, mister? Our boss will want some words with you when he gets back."

"Where is Mad Dog, anyway?" Bobbie Joe asked.

"Off with the girl, mademoiselle," DePue answered. "He is having a lot of fun with her."

Fargo's worst dread had come true. Lucille was being molested. "Some outlaws you are," he said in contempt.

DePue's head jerked up. "*Oui,* monsieur. We are the best. It is why we have lasted longer than anyone else. It is why we will go on stealing to our heart's content."

"Stealing is one thing," Fargo said. "Taking the woman was another."

"*Oui,* it was," the Cajun concurred, and laughed heartily.

Yoas swore. "I warned Mad Dog not to do it but he wouldn't listen. I warned him a posse would show up."

"We all expected the law to come after us," Mattox said. "But you are the one who brought them to our doorstep." His chuckle was reminiscent of a bear's growl. "Mad Dog won't be none too happy about that. He won't be happy at all."

As if he had been waiting for that very moment, a rider appeared off across the valley, trotting toward them.

"Speak of the devil!" Mattox declared. "Here he comes now. I can't wait. You know how much he likes surprises."

Plainly uneasy, Yoas shifted his weight from one leg to the next. "He will not be mad, not when it is her."

The rider came steadily on. He raised an arm and waved, seemed to stiffen, then lowered his arm and brought his mount to a gallop.

"Mad Dog has seen we have visitors," DePue said.

No one said anything after that. Judging by fidgeting and the tension on their faces, the three outlaws were worried. Mattox, whose fingers were as thick as railroad spikes and who looked strong enough to bend iron bars;

the short breed Yoas, who had already demonstrated how deadly he was; and the arrogant Cajun—all three were secretly scared of the man coming toward them, so scared they could not help betraying their fear.

Fargo did not know what he expected. A name like Mad Dog Terrell brought to mind the notion of a brutish monster, a man with the beastlike traits his name implied.

But names did not always match those they described. Fargo once knew a man named Shorty who was almost seven feet tall. A friend jokingly called the man that one day and the nickname stuck. There was a tavern keeper everyone called Bull who was as mild as a kitten. His nickname stemmed from the day he accidentally stepped in some bull droppings when he was growing up on the family farm. And there was a Crow Indian known as Four Ears who did not have any. The Blackfeet got hold of him one day and chopped them off. He escaped, taking his ears with him, and ever after carried them around in a pouch.

Fargo thought of them as the rider came to a stop. Mad Dog Terrell was nothing like his name suggested he would be.

For starters, Mad Dog wore a tailored suit that was the height of fashion in places like St. Louis and New Orleans. His black boots were polished, his black hat fairly new. His shirt, his pants, were spotlessly clean. His black leather holster was decorated with silver studs, his nickel-plated Colt had a pearl handle. As for brutish features, nothing could be further from the truth. Terrell was clean shaven, his face the kind that stopped women in their tracks. Fargo was often called handsome but Terrell was more so, just about the handsomest man Fargo ever saw. Everything about Terrell was flawless.

Except his eyes.

Mad Dog Terrell's were a rare shade of slate gray. They were not normal in another respect, as well: they had a piercing intensity about them. The only thing he could compare them to were the eyes of some crazed animal. The crazed eyes of a rabid dog, for instance. Terrell's eyes never changed, never became calm or ordinary. It was unnerving to gaze into those twin windows into the dark side of a twisted soul.

"Well, well, well." Mad Dog's voice was low and deep. "What have we here?"

"It is not my fault," Mattox declared.

"We have guests," DePue said with a suave smile. "The charming Mademoiselle Jentry has shown up out of the blue."

"I have eyes," Mad Dog said, and smiled at her. But his smile did not touch those strange eyes of his. "How do you do, Bobbie Joe? It is a pleasure to see you again."

"I am fine, Bruce. I hope you will forgive me for bein' here."

Fargo gave a mild start. No one, not even Deputy Gavin, knew Mad Dog Terrell's first name. But she did.

"Of course, my dear," Mad Dog told her. "But your presence raises questions." Those intense eyes fixed on Fargo. "So does yours, stranger. Since you undoubtedly know who I am, suppose you show you have manners and tell me who you are."

Fargo did.

"He is part of a posse out of Springfield," Bobbie Joe elaborated. "The scout the deputy brought along to track you."

"You don't say," Mad Dog said. "And you considerately brought him here so he can go back and bring the rest?"

"It is not like that. You know me better. I am on your side. I want to help you."

"How *did* you find our little sanctuary, by the way?" Mad Dog asked.

Yoas had been fidgeting as if ants were running amok under his clothes. Now he took a step toward Terrell and said in a strained voice, "She followed me, senor. I did as you wanted and left the note. I thought they were all sitting around a fire, talking it over, when I left."

"You never checked your back trail?"

"As God is my witness," Yoas said. "I am always cautious." He stopped and a look of shame came over him. "But I did not see them. They were too clever for me."

"My dear Jose," Mad Dog said. "You need not feel guilty. If that man had been trailing me, I would not have noticed, either."

"You never miss anything," Yoas said.

Mad Dog flashed even white teeth in a dazzling smile. "High praise, for which I thank you. But you must be unaware of who he is. Don't any of you know?"

Their blank expressions were answer enough. Mad Dog sighed and sadly shook his head. "I expect better of men who ride with me. I will overlook most any fault, but never stupidity." He pointed at Fargo. "You heard him mention his name. Don't you ever read newspapers? Or listen to saloon gossip? Mr. Fargo, gentlemen, is more than a common scout. They speak of him in the same breath as Kit Carson and Jim Bridger. He was in that shooting contest in Springfield a while back."

"The one with all the famous people?" Mattox asked.

"Yes, you thick-skulled lummox," Mad Dog confirmed. "He is dangerous, gentlemen. Very dangerous. So can any of you tell me why the only one holding a gun on him is Bobbie Joe?"

Just like that, DePue and Yoas and Mattox produced their revolvers and trained them on Fargo.

"Better, much better," Mad Dog said. Dismounting, he came over and held out his hand for Bobbie Joe to take. "Permit me to help you down."

"You sure spoil a girl," Bobbie Joe grinned, and giggled as he lowered her. "Such a gracious gentleman."

"Think nothing of it," Mad Dog said suavely. Still smiling, he slapped her across the face, slapped her so hard that she stumbled back against the dun and would have fallen had she not clutched the saddle.

"What was that for?" Bobbie Joe asked, more shocked than hurt.

"You called me by my first name," Mad Dog replied. "You know how I hate that." His smile faded as he turned toward Fargo and placed his hand on his pearl-handled Colt. "Now then. What are we to do with you?" He snapped the fingers of his other hand. "I know. I will be as gracious as Bobbie Joe claims, and leave it up to you." He paused. "How do you want to die?"

12

Mad Dog Terrell threw back his handsome head and laughed.

Fargo had never heard a laugh quite like it. Part bray, part screech, part snarl, and overall, tinged with a hint of something vile and vicious that lurked just below the surface. It was a laugh that would frighten children and raise gooseflesh on anyone scared of things that went bump in the night.

Bobbie Joe Jentry had regained her balance after being slapped, and now she took a step back, a hand rising to her throat. "Dear God. That is the first time I have ever heard you do that."

"So?" Mad Dog said, as if the sounds that issued from his throat were perfectly ordinary.

"Forget it," Bobbie Joe said, then, "Don't ever hit me again, do you hear? No one puts a hand on me."

"Is that so?" Mad Dog seemed about to hit her again but instead faced Fargo. "One thing at a time, my dear. What do you think? Should I have him staked out and skinned?"

"No," Bobbie Joe said.

"Tie him to a stake and burn him alive?"

"Not that, either."

"You sure are fussy about how people are killed," Mad Dog remarked.

"I don't want him harmed," Bobbie Joe said. "That isn't why I got the drop on him and brought him to you."

Mad Dog scratched his handsome chin. "Why did you, exactly? I am unclear on your motive."

"To give you and your friends time to get away. The posse won't get here for hours yet. By then you can be far away and safe."

"You want me to tuck tail and run?" Mad Dog made clucking sounds. "Surely you know me better than that?"

"Damn it, it is the smart thing to do," Bobbie Joe persisted. "Kill them and another, bigger, posse will be sent. The sheriff with fifty men instead of the deputy with three."

Mad Dog looked at his companions. "Did you hear her, boys? She wants us to run from a tin star and three peckerwoods. What do you say?"

Yoas answered first. "Do you even need to ask?"

"I say we kill them all," Mattox growled.

"I agree," DePue said. "If we run from so few, men will say we are yellow. We can not have that."

"Oh, God." Bobbie Joe looked from one to the other in horror. "I thought you would listen to reason."

"Me?" Mad Dog said, and uttered that unnatural laugh of his. "Our night together did not teach you much, did it?"

A pink tinge crept from Bobbie Joe's neck to her hairline.

Mad Dog gestured at Fargo, and switching moods in the blink of an eye, snapped, "Why isn't he tied? Must I do everything myself?"

With Yoas and DePue covering him, Fargo had no choice but to submit as Mattox bound his wrists in front of him. Mattox then clamped a hand on Fargo's shoulder, digging his nails in, and propelled Fargo toward the cabin door. Just when Fargo thought he would be slammed against it, Mattox stopped, opened it for him, and practically hurled him inside.

Fargo stumbled but did not fall. It took a few seconds for his eyes to adjust to the gloom. To his amazement, the interior was nicely furnished. He would never have guessed, from the burlap on the window. There was an oak table and four chairs and a rug on the floor. In the corner stood a stove and along one wall ran a counter with neatly stacked cooking utensils. On another wall hung, of all things, a painting of a young woman in a flowing dress. A door opened into another room. Through it Fargo could see beds. Not cots, not blankets spread on the floor, but honest-to-God beds.

"Like it?" Mad Dog asked. "We only stop here on our way in and out of the mountains. A relay station, you might say."

Mattox pushed Fargo into a chair so hard, the chair nearly tipped over. Fargo took the treatment calmly, which seemed to anger Mattox. "Nothing to say, mister?"

"Do you have any whiskey?"

Mattox blinked. "We are fixing to do you in and all you want is a drink? And people say I am dumb!"

Mad Dog sank into a chair across the table. "If our guest wants a drink, get him a drink." He patted the table. "Bobbie Joe, why don't you sit here next to me so we can get reacquainted?"

Yoas went to sit but Mad Dog kicked the chair out from under him. "What do you think you are doing? You led them here. You will mount up and backtrack and make damn sure the posse isn't close behind. One surprise a day is my limit."

As meekly as a lamb, and with a parting glare at Bobbie Joe and Fargo, the swarthy killer stalked out.

DePue had hung back near the door. "What do you want me to do? Go with Yoas?"

"No. I want you to saddle the horses and get the pack animals ready. We might need to fan the breeze in a hurry."

Fargo waited until the door closed to ask, "Where is the girl you took from the stage? She'd better be alive."

"Lucy?" Mad Dog said, his eyebrows arching. "What is she to you?"

"I've met her," Fargo revealed. "We had supper together."

"Small world, isn't it?" Mad Dog said, and chuckled.

"I took her riding this morning. We had a marvelous time."

"You left her out there?" To Fargo that boded ill. He imagined her battered and broken, lying in a pool of blood.

"I advise you to talk about something else," Mad Dog said.

"In that case"—Fargo bobbed his chin at Bobbie Joe Jentry—"how does she fit in?"

"I can answer for myself," Bobbie Joe said.

Mad Dog grinned. "Why don't you, my dear? Tell him everything. He must be burning with curiosity."

Bobbie Joe stared at the table. "I already told him some of it. How you and me met that time my kin and me were camped out by Devil's Lake."

"You should have seen her," Mad Dog said to Fargo. "Standing in the lake with the water up to her knees, and holding a rod in one hand and a string of fish in the other. Who could ignore so ravishing a vision?"

"Don't poke fun," Bobbie Joe said.

"Her sisters and cousins are trolls compared to her," Mad Dog said. "She took my breath away." He covered her hand with his. "The feeling was mutual. She told me I was the prettiest man she ever saw."

Mattox laughed. Fargo expected Terrell to say something but he didn't.

"I didn't say you were pretty," Bobbie Joe said. "I called you the handsomest man I ever saw."

"And you couldn't believe I was interested in you," Mad Dog teased. He winked at Fargo. "You never saw anyone so shy in your life. She did not have much experience with men."

"Don't," Bobbie Joe said.

"Too late, my dear," Mad Dog responded. Then, to Fargo, "By the end of the night she was hopelessly in love with me. When we parted, I vowed to return for her one day and take her for my wife."

Bobbie Joe clasped his hand in both of hers. "You promised. We pledged our love for as long as we draw breath."

"Yes, well," Mad Dog said, and coughed. "A man will promise most anything to get up a woman's petticoats. Or, in your case, in her britches."

Bobbie Joe jerked back as if he had slapped her again. "What are you sayin'?"

"Only that while it was sweet of you to be so worried about my welfare that you betrayed the posse you are part of, you should not take it for granted that our vows that night are binding."

Fargo almost felt sorry for her. The dawning truth, the hurt, stunned her. She seemed to shrivel in her chair.

"Please, no."

"Oh, come now," Mad Dog chided. "Be adult about this. We had a nice night together. That is all."

"But we—" Bobbie Joe began, and did not finish.

"Yes, we did," Mad Dog said, chortling. "And I must say you were delightful. What you lacked in experience you more than made up for with enthusiasm."

"Damn you."

"Let's not start that. No one forced you to lie with me. You came to me of your own free will and shared your body because you wanted to."

Tears moistened Bobbie Joe's eyes. "You said you loved me. You said that you would give up your outlaw ways one day and we would live together as man and wife."

"You can't be so naive as to think I meant it?" Mad Dog responded. "Good God. Tie myself to one woman? The notion is preposterous."

A tear trickled from a corner of Bobbie Joe's eye.

Mad Dog Terrell did the last thing a man should do when a woman professes her love; he laughed. "You did! You truly did! Oh, how marvelous. I am flattered, my dear. But honestly. You need to grow up. You need to see things as they are and not as you fancy them to be."

Bobbie Joe coughed and had to try twice to speak. "And how are they between us, exactly? Since you don't love me, do you like me? Even a little bit? Or not at all?"

"There is no such thing as love. Men say they care for

a woman to have their way with them, and when they have had their way, they go on to another woman and lie to her so she will part her legs."

"That is all I ever was to you?"

"How could you expect to be anything else?" Mad Dog glibly replied. "As best I can recall, we met in the middle of a hot summer's afternoon, and by two in the morning I had your britches down. Does that sound like true love or lust?"

"But I thought— That is, you were—" Bobbie Joe stuttered. With a visible effort she gained control of her emotions. "So you do not love me and every word you told me was a lie and I was a fool to come here to warn you. Is that how it is?"

"Not everything was a lie," Mad Dog corrected her. "When I said you had a fine body, I meant it."

"God," Bobbie Joe said softly.

"There is no Almighty, either, so don't bring religion into this. We shared a night together and now I am done with you." Mad Dog grinned, and put his hand on hers. "Unless you want to spend another night together."

Bobbie Joe shook from head to toe, then yanked her hand away. "What did I ever see in you?"

"What every woman sees. The best-looking man alive," Mad Dog boasted.

"You are a pig."

"No insults, remember?" Mad Dog said. "Be adult about this."

"*Adult?*" Bobbie Joe exploded. "Is that what you call it? You lie, you steal a girl's virtue, and then you have the gall to say I am actin' childish?"

"You are," Mad Dog said coldly. "As for your virtue, if I truly was the first, it will be something to brag about. I rarely get to poke a virgin."

Bobbie Joe came out of her chair as if hurled out of it. Her right hand was a streak. She raked her nails across Terrell's face, across his cheek from his brow to his chin, leaving bloody furrows when she drew her hand back to do it again.

"Grab her!" Mad Dog snarled, and seized her wrist.

Bobbie Joe's other hand flew to the hilt of her knife but by then Mattox was behind her chair. His huge hands closed on her like twin vises, pinning her arms to her sides. She struggled but she was completely helpless in the giant's grip.

While all this had been going on, Fargo had been busy. He had lowered his hands under the table and hiked his leg so he could reach his Arkansas toothpick, nestled snug in its ankle sheath. Then, reversing his grip, he had cut at the rope, careful to move his fingers but not his arms. The double-edged toothpick was razor sharp, but the rope was thick and it took some doing. He had it halfway through when Mattox seized Bobbie Joe.

Mad Dog touched his fingers to his cheek and then stared at the drops of blood on his fingertips, his jaw muscles twitching. "You bitch. You miserable little bitch." Rising, he moved to a mirror on the far wall. "Look at what you have done to me! I could be scarred."

"I hope you are!" Bobbie Joe shrilly cried. "I hope I spoiled your looks so you won't be as handsome for the next poor female you take advantage of!"

Fargo had no way of preventing what happened next. Not with his wrists still bound.

Whirling, Mad Dog Terrell uttered a howl of rage worthy of his namesake. In three long strides he was at the table. Gripping Bobbie Joe by the forearm, he hollered at Mattox, "Let go of her!" and wrenched her out of the chair. She tried to claw him again but Mad Dog blocked the blow, drew back his fist, and punched her in the stomach.

Doubling over, Bobbie Joe wheezed and sputtered and staggered a few steps. She went red in the face and could not catch her breath.

"Claw me, will you?" Mad Dog rasped, and struck her again, this time on the temple. He did not hold back. He did not go easy on her because she was a woman. He hit her with all his might and Bobbie Joe Jentry collapsed in an unconscious sprawl.

It took every ounce of will Fargo possessed to stay in his chair and keep cutting at the rope.

Mattox was grinning in delight. "Want me to stomp on her? Break a few ribs and such?"

"Lay a hand on her," Mad Dog snarled, "and you die." Stooping, he cupped her chin and violently shook her head. "This one is mine. No one is to touch her but me."

Fargo could not stay silent. "This is how you repay her for trying to help you?"

Unfurling, Mad Dog hissed like a riled snake. "I didn't ask the cow to bring you here. She did it on her own." He nudged Bobbie Joe with a toe. "She has only herself to blame if she ends up sharing the same grave as you."

"What do you have in mind?" Fargo asked. Not that he cared. He was stalling to buy time to free his arms.

Mad Dog Terrell laughed that inhuman laugh of his. "Let me put it this way: I would not want to be you."

13

"Let me strangle him, Mad Dog," Mattox requested. "You know how much I like to strangle things." His dark eyes glittered at the prospect and he licked his thick lips.

"Strangling is too quick. I want them both to suffer a good long while before they die."

Fargo was almost through the rope. He dared not look but he could feel the strands giving way. A few more and he would have it.

Then hooves drummed and voices were raised, Yoas yelling something and DePue answering. Mad Dog and Mattox turned toward the front door just as it opened, framing the swarthy half-breed.

"You are supposed to be backtracking these two," Terrell said, with a jab of his thumb at Fargo and Bobbie Joe.

"I got as far as the end of the valley," Yoas said, "and I spotted the posse coming down through the timber to the northeast."

Fargo was surprised. Deputy Gavin had agreed to stay put until he found the outlaws and reported back.

"Did they see you?"

"I don't think so. I came back by way of the stream and did not break cover until I was close to the cabin."

Mad Dog had a habit of scratching his chin when he was thinking. "How many are there?"

"It is as the woman told you," Yoas answered. "There are only four."

And one of them, Fargo grimly reflected, was in handcuffs. He had a sinking feeling that unless he did something, and did it quick, the posse was going to ride smack into an ambush.

"I figure it will be half an hour yet before they get here," Yoas had gone on.

"Does DePue have the horses saddled?" Mad Dog Terrell asked.

"He was saddling the last one as I rode up," Yoas answered.

"Good. Tell him to leave the packhorses in the corral for now. We want the posse to think we are here. I will be right out."

"As you wish," Yoas obediently replied, and dashed off.

Mattox clenched and unclenched his enormous hands. "We are setting a trap?"

"We are," Mad Dog confirmed. "Find some rope and tie Bobbie Joe. Gag her, too, to be on the safe side." He turned toward the table.

Fargo stopped cutting. Pinching the hilt of the Arkansas toothpick against his palm, he slid the blade up his sleeve so the knife was less likely to be noticed.

"On your feet," Mad Dog commanded.

"What about Lucille Sparks?"

"What about her?" Mad Dog retorted. "She is none of your concern and never was."

"Is she still alive?" Fargo wanted to learn.

Mad Dog started around the table, his hand on his pearl-handled Colt, his handsome features twisted in fury. "You don't listen very well, do you?"

"You can't blame me for worrying about her," Fargo said, standing with his wrists pressed against his buckskins.

Those peculiar eyes of Mad Dog's were fixed so intently on him, that for a few seconds Fargo thought Terrell was about to draw and gun him down where he stood. But Mad Dog merely took his hand off the Colt and said harshly, "Outside. And don't try anything or we kill the cow."

Mattox looked up from binding Bobbie Joe. "I can snap her neck if he gives us any trouble."

"No. I kill her, remember?" Mad Dog said. "But you can cut her nose off if you want if he acts up."

Fargo dared not make his move. Not yet. He moved around the opposite side of the table from Terrell and over to the door. The moment he stepped outside, Yoas was there with his six-shooter out.

"Are you thinking about your friends, gringo? You should be. They are not long for this world." Yoas wagged his revolver. "Over to the horses. I will be right behind you."

Fargo gazed to the northeast but he did not spot the posse. He came to the Ovaro and reached for the saddle horn.

"Not yet," Yoas said. "I will tell you when."

Fargo turned. "I have been meaning to ask. Was that you who took a shot at me back at Dawson's Corners?"

"*Sí,*" Yoas said. "Mad Dog sent me to watch and see if a posse came after us, and to slow them down if they did. I saw you and the woman walk off into the woods and figured I might as well start with you." He scowled. "The damn shadows spoiled my aim."

"That's how you like to do it, isn't it? From a distance, so you are good and safe."

Yoas took a half step toward him. "Call me a coward again and I shoot you, Mad Dog or no Mad Dog."

"One day he will turn on you, you know," Fargo told him. "He only cares about himself."

Feet swished the high grass, and DePue was there, smirking. "That is where you are wrong, *mon ami. Oui,* Terrell is not as other men, but he values us. He has saved each of our lives at one time or another. Mine, when he shot a man who was about to shoot me in the back."

"One day you will be of no more use to him, and that will be that," Fargo predicted.

"Ignore him," Yoas said to DePue. "He is trying to turn us against Mad Dog and it will not work."

"No, it will not," DePue assured Fargo. "We have ridden with him too long. He has earned our loyalty."

"You are jackasses."

DePue's expression hardened. "That kind of talk, monsieur, will only put you under the ground that much sooner."

Mad Dog came out of the cabin. Behind him lumbered Mattox, Bobbie Joe slung over a shoulder like a sack of flour. "Mount up," the former commanded.

Exercising care that the toothpick did not slip out of his sleeve, Fargo forked leather and lifted the reins. He still did not see any sign of Gavin and the others.

With a wave of an arm, Mad Dog Terrell rode west at a gallop. Mattox, DePue and Yoas flanked Fargo, ensuring he did not try to get away. Not that he would so long as they had Bobbie Joe. Soon they came to the edge of the timber and Mad Dog slowed.

Looking back, Fargo saw that the cabin was just out of rifle range. He breathed a little easier but his relief proved short-lived.

Mad Dog entered the trees and immediately drew rein. "Shuck your rifles," he instructed the others, yanking his own from the scabbard. "Our tracks are plain enough that the posse should come after us. When they do, we will shoot them to pieces."

"I like how you think," Mattox chortled.

"All you ever want to do is kill," Yoas said to him.

The monster grinned. "Killing is the most fun I know. And you are a fine one to talk. I have yet to see you spare anyone when you had the chance."

DePue was checking that his rifle was loaded. "We all like to kill. It is the glue that holds us together."

"I never thought of it like that, Creole," Mattox said as he plopped Bobbie Joe belly down over his saddle.

"It is *Cajun*, you lunkhead," DePue sniped. "Will you ever get it right?"

Mad Dog was wrapping the reins to his mount around a low limb. "Enough damn chatter. You are worse than a bunch of women." He crooked a finger at Fargo. "Come along. You will want to see this."

Fargo had no desire to witness the posse being wiped out but he followed. He was tempted to bury the toothpick between Terrell's shoulder blades but both Yoas and Mattox were behind him and would blast him if he did.

Crouching next to an oak, Mad Dog pointed at a spot a few feet from him and said, "Sit."

Fargo did.

"The rest of you spread out. No one is to shoot until I do. Anyone does, and they answer to me."

Quiet descended, except for the usual sounds of the forest: sparrows chirping, an irate squirrel venting its spleen, the screech of a hawk in the distance. Fargo could see the upper half of the cabin over the high grass that covered the valley floor. He started to rise to his knees to see better and instantly Terrell swung toward him and cocked the hammer of his rifle.

"What do you think you're doing? Sit back down and stay down."

Fargo sank back. "You are making a mistake. Kill them and another posse will come, just like Bobbie Joe warned you. Enough men and guns that you won't stand a prayer."

"No one has caught me yet," Mad Dog bragged. "No one ever will. I know these mountains better than anyone. I have been all over them."

"You can't escape the law forever."

"I don't need to do it that long," Mad Dog said. "Only for another twenty to thirty years. By then I will be so old, I will be gumming my food, and it won't matter."

"What did you do with Lucille?"

"Back to her again, are you? I told you she was none of your concern. Forget about her."

"I can't," Fargo said.

Mad Dog frowned. "I would laugh in your face if you weren't so pathetic." His frown deepened and his mouth twitched. "I can't wait to whittle on you. I truly can't."

Off across the valley, in the trees fringing the stream, riders appeared. Fargo noticed them right away but Terrell was looking at him and did not see them. In order to delay their discovery, Fargo asked, "Why do you hate me so much?"

"It is not just you," Mad Dog said bitterly. "It is your kind."

"I have a kind?"

"Law-abiding sheep. People who don't mind being told what to do. People who spend their whole lives living by rules others set down. That's not for me. I do as I please, when I please."

"If everyone thought like you do, it wouldn't be safe to walk the streets," Fargo remarked.

Mad Dog was staring at the ground. "I never have liked being made to do things. Even as a kid, when my mother would tell me to clean my room and go sweep out the barn, I wanted to take an ax to her head."

"You had a mother?"

Mad Dog's head snapped up and his eyes became slits. "You will be a week dying. More, if I do it right. Before the end comes you will beg me to put you out of your misery."

"I wouldn't count on me begging," Fargo said. The posse was in full view. Deputy Gavin, Old Charley and Foley had fanned out and were converging on the cabin. Lynch Spicer, still handcuffed, hung back.

"They all say that until I start to work on them," Mad Dog mentioned. "Usually all it takes is for me to pop out an eyeball and show it to them and they blubber like babies."

Fargo wished the posse would dismount and advance on foot. They were ridiculously easy targets on horseback. Gavin should have waited until dark. Then it hit him. Gavin had thrown caution to the wind because the deputy was worried about Bobbie Joe and him.

"I like to cut people up. They call it torture but I call it amusement. I have been doing it since I was seven. My first was a rabbit, a bunny my mother had in a hutch. She made me help her shuck peas, so later, when she was knitting in her rocking chair, I took her butcher knife from the kitchen, snuck out to the hutch, and carved that bunny to bits." Mad Dog smiled wistfully at the memory. "I cut off its ears first. For years I had them as keepsakes."

Fargo glanced across the valley. The posse was halfway to the cabin. If only he could keep Terrell talking a while longer. "When did you switch from rabbits to people?"

"I killed my first man when I was ten. Between the rabbit and him were a lot of other animals. Dogs, cats, a cow, a rooster, a duck." Mad Dog laughed. "The duck quacked every time I stuck my knife into her. I chopped off both her legs and both her wings and she still went on quacking. It was comical."

"It was sick," Fargo said.

Mad Dog sighed. "I wouldn't expect someone like you to understand. Sheep never do."

Fargo racked his brain for something else to say or ask that would keep Terrell distracted. But just then DePue whispered Mad Dog's name and pointed toward the cabin.

One look, and Terrell gnashed his teeth in anger. "You clever bastard. Nice try, but it didn't work." He wedged the stock of his rifle to his shoulder. "All you did was buy them a few more minutes of life." Sighting down the barrel, he smiled. "I bet you ten dollars I can hit the tin star on that law dog's vest."

Fargo coiled his legs to spring. He could not sit there and let it happen. He must do what he could, even if it cost him his life. Sliding the toothpick from under his sleeve, he eased up onto the balls of his feet. If he could kill Terrell, if he could grab Terrell's rifle, he stood a chance of saving Gavin and the others. Lancing the toothpick at Terrell's neck, he sprang.

"Look out!"

The bellow came from Mattox. Mad Dog spun. Steel rang on steel as the toothpick glanced off the rifle barrel. Fargo was thrown off balance but he instantly recovered and stabbed at the outlaw's gut. By rights he should have opened Mad Dog's belly but a blow to the back of his head nearly pitched him onto his face. Dimly, he heard Mattox bellow something else. A second blow drove him to his hands and knees. He tried to get back up but his senses were reeling. The bright glare of sunlight was fading to black. Words filtered through.

"Thanks. He almost had me. Now let's pick us off a posse. Aim for the chest and make every shot count."

Fargo made one more attempt to rise and then the void claimed him.

14

A swaying sensation was proof to Fargo he was still alive. He struggled up through a mental fog and was rewarded for his effort with waves of pain. His head throbbed fit to burst. He opened his eyes and found he had been thrown over his saddle, belly down. Not only that, his wrists and ankles were bound. By craning his neck he saw that Mattox was leading the pinto by the reins. A glance back showed Yoas leading the horse that bore Bobbie Joe. DePue brought up the rear.

Fargo tried to speak but all that came out was a dry hack. He needed a drink of water.

"This one is awake!" Yoas hollered.

Hooves thudded and a shadow fell across Fargo. "Clever of you to have that ankle blade. I don't see many of those," Mad Dog Terrell said.

"Are they all dead?" Fargo croaked.

"We couldn't find the old geezer but we found blood where he fell. The rest were shot to ribbons."

Fargo closed his eyes.

"Don't take it so hard," Mad Dog said. "Better them than you. You get to breathe a while yet." He chuckled. "The one with the handcuffs on was still alive when we found him. You should have heard him squeal! He was more amusing than that bunny."

"He was the son of a judge," Fargo mentioned.

"Well, now he is maggot bait. Why was he wearing cuffs?"

Fargo explained. His head was slowly clearing. He was

glad to be alive but now he no longer had the toothpick. He must rely on his wits, and they had not been of much use the past few hours.

"That boy was a fool to ever leave Springfield," Mad Dog commented. "But that is what he gets for letting someone tell him what he should do. If that lawman had asked me to join a posse, I would have told him to go to hell."

"You sure love to talk about yourself."

"And you must love to hurt or you wouldn't keep on prodding me." Mad Dog gigged his mount.

Fargo was left alone with his thoughts, and they were glum. Deputy Gavin, dead. Kleb, dead. Foley, dead. Spicer, dead. Old Charley wounded and probably lying in the brush somewhere, dying. Bobbie Joe, a captive. Lucille Sparks, apparently dead after being raped by Mad Dog. Everything that could go wrong had gone wrong. All that was left was for Terrell to kill Bobbie Joe and him, and that would be that.

Fargo raised his head and gazed about. They were winding through some of the most rugged country yet, mountainous terrain, marked by steep slopes and thick forest. Compared to the Rocky Mountains, with their snow-mantled peaks towering miles into the sky, Missouri's mountains were puny, but then, so was every range east of the Mississippi. Missouri's mountains, though, made up in one respect what they lacked in height. Water was scarce in the Rockies. Here there were creeks and streams and rivers and lakes aplenty, more water in a hundred square miles than there was to be found in a thousand square miles of the much drier Rockies, and thanks to all that water, far thicker vegetation.

It was brought to Fargo's mind when the outlaws came to a fast flowing stream and hugged the bank as it cascaded into a gorge. High stone ramparts blocked out the sun, plunging the bottom in gloom. The temperature dropped a few degrees. Cold spray from the collision of rushing water and partially submerged boulders filled the air with a fine chill mist.

The outlaws stuck to the left wall. Soon they neared

a bend. Instead of going around it, they rode straight at what Fargo took to be the shadowed base. But appearances were deceiving, especially when he was hanging upside down over a horse.

Long ago, when the water level was higher, the stream had accomplished what no amount of digging could ever do; it had worn a cave, and more, out of the solid rock.

As best Fargo could determine, the mouth was thirty feet wide and twenty feet high. The outlaws had been here before. Charred embers from a former fire was the first clue. The second, provisions stacked along the cave wall.

Mattox climbed down and shambled to the pinto. Fargo winced as iron fingers dug into his back and he was lifted bodily from the saddle and dumped on the hard stone. He tried to cushion the drop with his shoulder and regretted it when he spiked with agony.

DePue set to work kindling the fire.

Yoas dragged Bobbie Joe over by her feet and left her lying next to Fargo. She tried to kick the breed but he nimbly skipped aside, laughing. "I hate them," she said softly. "I hate all of them."

"Does that include Mad Dog?" Fargo asked.

"Him most of all. I loved him. I honestly and truly loved him. And this is how he treats me." Bobbie Joe rose on an elbow and puffed at hair that had fallen across her face.

"He plans to treat us a lot worse."

Bobbie Joe glared at the outlaws, who were stripping saddles and saddle blankets, then wriggled closer to Fargo. "Listen. There has to be a way out of this fix. I don't want to die."

"That makes two of us," Fargo said.

"With our wrists and our ankles tied, there is not much we can do. But there has to be *something*."

Fargo had been noting the cave floor. "It depends on how much time we have." If Terrell started carving on them right away, they were plumb out of luck and life.

"You have an idea that can save our hides?" Bobbie Joe eagerly asked.

"I might. But we need time," Fargo said, and was puzzled when she twisted and yelled for Mad Dog.

Terrell wore the grin of a man who had the upper hand and relished having it. "What can I do for you, my dear?"

"I want to haggle."

The puzzlement was contagious. Mad Dog's brow furrowed and he scratched his chin. "Over what?"

"My life. Fargo's too. I want to barter for them if you will do so in good faith."

Mad Dog glanced at Fargo. "What is she babbling about? What does she have to barter with?"

"When she tells you we will both know," Fargo said, eyeing Bobbie Joe quizzically.

"What do you say?" she asked Terrell. "Will you give me your word to do as we agree?"

"Woman, you try my patience," Mad Dog warned. "You have nothing to barter with. Your lives are mine to take as I see fit."

"I have one thing to barter," Bobbie Joe said. "Me."

"How is that again?"

Bobbie Joe rolled onto her back. "You heard me. I am offerin' you me. I will treat you to a night like we had at the lake if you will let Fargo and me go in the mornin'."

His eyes widening in comprehension, Mad Dog said, "Let me be sure I have this straight. You want to barter your body for your life?"

"My life and his, yes."

Mad Dog's eerie laugh peeled loud in the cave. He laughed and laughed, his hands on his legs, until he had laughed himself out and was gasping for air. "You are a wonder, Bobbie Joe Jentry. No woman has ever done this before. Most would rather give up their life than give up their womanhood."

"I already gave it up to you once," Bobbie Joe said. "A second time won't bother me much."

"You take it for granted I want you a second time," Mad Dog said. "And you forget that I don't need to barter for your body. I can take it. I can do whatever I want with you and there is not a damn thing you can do about it."

Bobbie Joe was not intimidated. "Yes, you can have your way with me. But it won't be the same. I will lie here like a bump on a log and you won't get half the enjoyment."

"You still ask too much," Mad Dog said. "As fine a body as you have, it is not enough."

"How about a delay, then?" Bobbie Joe asked. "Will it keep me alive until dawn?"

Mad Dog roved an appreciative gaze over the shapely contours of her figure. "It might, yes. It just might at that. But there are conditions."

"Name them."

"You don't lie there like a bump on a log, as you put it. You show some fire, some spunk. And we do it with your hands tied."

"How can I get into the spirit of things if I can't move my arms?"

"Oh, I am sure you can think of something," Mad Dog smirked. "But I am not a fool. I know you would slit my throat if you could, or put a slug in my brain. So your wrists stay bound."

"Very well," Bobbie Joe said. "Anything else?"

"Not that I can think of at the moment. I will be back in five minutes to take you to my sleeping quarters."

"Your what?"

Mad Dog pointed at a dark patch on the rear wall. "The cave goes back a ways, and there are nooks off the tunnel. The boys and me each have our own little cubby." Hooking his thumbs in his belt, he strolled toward the fire.

Fargo had been silent long enough. "You don't need to do this. There has to be another way."

"If you know what it is, I am listenin'," Bobbie Joe said. "If you don't, then this will buy you that time you need." She bowed her head and shuddered. "The notion of him touchin' me turns my stomach but it can't be helped."

Fargo lay there trying to think of a better ruse, but for the life of him he couldn't.

When Mad Dog returned he was in good spirits. Whistling as he strolled up to them, he leered hungrily down at Bobbie Joe. "Are you ready, girl? If you have changed your mind, now is the time to tell me. It will only make me mad if you change it later, and when I am mad, I am not very nice."

"Just ask his bunny," Fargo said, and regretted it when Terrell lashed out with a boot and caught him in the ribs. His whole side exploded with torment but it could have been worse.

"Why did you do that?" Bobbie Joe asked the outlaw. "What was that about a rabbit?"

"It was your friend's idea of humor," Mad Dog growled. "The next time I will kick in his teeth." Bending, he grabbed her arms and hoisted her onto her backside. "Yoas, get over here with that fancy dagger you are so fond of."

The breed was quick to obey. He cut the rope around Bobbie Joe's ankles and went to cut the rope around her wrists.

"Leave that one be," Mad Dog directed. "While I am in the back having my pokes, I want you and the others to keep a close eye on our famous marksman. Not that he can do anything, trussed up like a turkey. But better safe than buried." He pushed Bobbie Joe toward the tunnel. "Off you go, darling. I will be right behind you, so behave."

Yoas chuckled and winked at Fargo. "I wish it was me having the senorita. But I will get to later, after he is done."

"What do you mean?"

"Mad Dog promised Mattox and DePue and me that we could all take a turn before he kills her."

Fargo inwardly vowed that if it was the last thing he ever did, he would see to it that that never happened.

Yoas was feeling talkative. "The last female I had was a pretty young hellcat who made the mistake of being married to an idiot. They were in a covered wagon, heading for St. Joseph, and were camped all by themselves out in the middle of nowhere. Mattox strangled the man while the rest of us took turns with the wife." Grinning at the memory, Yoas ambled over to his companions.

At last Fargo was alone. He looked about him. Earlier he had noticed that the cave floor was not flat and smooth but dotted with upthrust fingers of rock. None were more than two or three inches high. Many had rough edges. The nearest was a few feet to his right.

Hooking his elbows under him, Fargo levered toward it. He went slowly so as not to draw unwanted attention. Mattox, DePue and Yoas were drinking coffee and talking, and except for occasional glances in his direction, they ignored him.

So short a distance, but Fargo consumed minutes crawling to the spike he had selected. He contrived to rest his forearms so the baby stalagmite was between them. Then he commenced sawing back and forth. The rock chafed and hurt his wrists but he persevered. He had plenty of incentive: the thought of Bobbie Joe in Mad Dog's arms.

Fargo wondered where his toothpick had gotten to. The last he saw of it was when he tried to stab Terrell and nearly had his skull caved in by Mattox. Either one of the outlaws had it or it was lying off in the forest somewhere, he reckoned.

Fargo did not know how long it had taken them to ride to the cave. He could not see the sun from where he lay, and he could not tell what time it was. Late afternoon was his best guess. Mad Dog had gotten an early start on his lovemaking.

Fargo was so engrossed in freeing himself, and in thinking of what he would like to do to Terrell when he got his hands on him, that he belatedly realized he was not alone. He immediately stopped moving his wrists.

"What are you doing, senor?" Yoas asked.

"Just lying here," Fargo answered, looking up.

"You have moved from where you were," Yoas observed. "After Mad Dog told you not to. Why did you disobey?"

"These damn ropes have cut off my circulation," Fargo lied. "I needed to move a little to stop the pain."

Yoas bought it. He removed his wide-brimmed black hat and ran his fingers through his shock of hair. "Very well. This time you are excused. But do not move again unless you ask us first. Savvy?"

"I savvy," Fargo assured him. He lay meek and docile until the small man was hunkered by the fire. Then he resumed slashing. Twice the jagged edge bit into his flesh and not the rope. But presently his arms were free. Smiling, he was about to sit up when a huge hand fell on his shoulder.

"What the hell are you up to?"

15

Fargo calmly stared up into Mattox's brutish face. "What are you talking about?" He was careful to lie so his wrists were under him.

"I have been watching you," Mattox said. "You have been wriggling and jiggling like a worm on a hook."

"I told Yoas a while ago and now I will tell you," Fargo said. "The ropes are cutting off my circulation. If I don't move my arms they start to hurt."

"You poor baby," Mattox guffawed, and straightened. "I bet right about now you are sorry you ever joined that posse."

"I am sorry they didn't kill all of you instead of the other way around," Fargo said.

Mattox's grin evaporated. "It's not smart to make me angry. Mad Dog isn't the only one who would kill you as soon as look at you." He motioned at the others. "That's why he picked us. Not everyone can ride with Mad Dog Terrell."

Fargo absorbed the revelation. "He doesn't let anyone in who wants to join up with him?"

"Hell, no. Mad Dog has his standards. He only takes those who are a lot like him. Natural born killers, you might say."

Fargo had never heard of such a thing, and said so.

"Mad Dog only wants men who don't mind spilling blood. Only those with at least ten killings to their credit. DePue, yonder, has exactly ten. Me, a couple more than that. Yoas, I think he has planted upwards of twenty.

Then there is Mad Dog himself. His tally is better than fifty."

"That many?" Fargo said skeptically.

"Mad Dog says killing is in his blood. Nothing gives him as much pleasure except maybe lying with a woman, and once he told me even that is a close second."

"You sound as if you admire him."

"I sure do," Mattox declared. "Mad Dog might be rough on us at times, but he looks out for us, and keeps us from making mistakes that would get us caught."

"And all the killing?" Fargo said.

"Haven't you heard a word I've been saying? Killing is what we live for. All of us. We like it so much, we will never stop this side of the grave." Mattox glowed with delight.

Fargo said nothing. He had met men like them before. The frontier crawled with renegades, outcasts and cutthroats, society's dregs, as a newspaper called them, badmen who liked being bad. They lived by the gun and by the knife, and thought no more of taking human life than most people thought of taking the life of a fly.

It was ironic. A lot was made about Indians in the newspapers, about how the redman was a heathen savage who loved to count coup on whites. But the truth was that most of the hostile tribes were only defending their territory and their loved ones from white invaders. To them, killing was a matter of survival. White outlaws, on the other hand, robbed and raped and killed because that was their nature. They were not protecting their families or their homes. They were doing it for *themselves*. It was an important distinction the newspapers failed to mention.

Mattox was speaking again. "I don't envy you none, mister. When Mad Dog is done with that filly he will start in on you, and I have seen him do things that would curl your hair."

"You like to watch him, don't you?"

"Of course." Mattox laughed. "We all do. He is so good at it. He does things I would never think of."

"You can't get away with this forever," Fargo said, wishing the giant would go so he could free his legs.

113

"Who says we can't?"

"Every outlaw is caught sooner or later. Few live to old age unless they are in prison."

Mattox snorted. "Talk like that doesn't scare me none. I like how we live, I like what we do, and I will go on doing it for as long as I am breathing. Whether I am bucked out in gore tomorrow or ten years from now, it is all the same to me."

"I hope it is tomorrow."

"That is some mouth you have on you," Mattox growled. "I can't wait until Mad Dog slices off your lips and cuts out your tongue. Then you won't be so uppity." Pivoting on a boot heel, he lumbered away.

Finally, Fargo thought, and shifted around so the spike was rubbing the rope that bound his ankles. He was facing the fire. Whenever the three killers were not looking, he moved his legs. Back and forth, back and forth, over and over, until his ankles and hips ached. Suddenly the rope parted. Fargo winced as the rock dug into his skin.

Decision time. Fargo wanted to go after Bobbie Joe. But even if he reached the tunnel undetected, the three by the fire were bound to notice he was missing and come after him. He had to do something about them first.

Just then, as if Providence was taking a hand, Yoas shot to his feet and turned toward the mouth of the cave. "What was that?"

"I didn't hear anything," Mattox said.

"Qu'est-ce que c'est?" DePue asked.

"Speak English, senor," Yoas said. He had his hand on his revolver and was staring up the gorge, the way they had come.

"What is it you think you heard?" Mattox asked.

"A horse, maybe. A hoof hitting rock." The breed moved closer to the entrance. "I think we should take a look."

"You are hearing things," Mattox said. "No one else knows about this place."

Yoas took several steps. "You forget, you big ox. One person does. But it could be anyone. I say we go see."

With an exaggerated sigh, DePue rose. "I guess we should. Mad Dog won't like it if we have uninvited guests and do nothing." He drew his revolver.

Mattox set down his tin cup. "Have it your way. We will have a look-see. But when we don't find anyone, remember it was me who said it was a waste of our time."

Fargo grinned at his turn of luck. Another minute, and the three were out of the cave and had disappeared. Rising, he ran to the fire. Their saddles and saddlebags lay scattered about. He searched but there was no sign of his Henry or the Colt or toothpick. He went to where the supplies were stacked but his weapons were not there, either.

Fargo swore. He did not have any more time to waste. Yoas, Mattox and DePue could be back any moment. He plunged into the tunnel and was swallowed by darkness. He passed a dark opening on his right, another on his left. From neither came any suggestion of life or movement. Then, up ahead, a pale glow beckoned. He slowed, moving silently now, the hunter and not the hunted.

An angry voice reached him. "—tired of your stalling. Either we do it or we don't, and if we don't, I will whip you within an inch of your life."

"A girl likes a little romance," Bobbie Joe said. "Give me another drink and sweet-talk me some and we will get to it."

"You have already had two drinks," Mad Dog criticized, "and I have talked myself damn near hoarse. Off with your clothes, woman."

A stone arch separated the tunnel from a small chamber. On one side were Terrell's personal effects. Near the back wall was an overturned barrel, on top of which a candle burned. On the right, blankets had been spread. Mad Dog was on his knees, glaring at Bobbie Joe, who sat with her back to the wall, holding an empty glass.

"You could at least be nice. It is not easy for me."

Mad Dog stabbed a finger at her. "*You* are the one

115

who wanted to barter her body for her life. If you did not think you could do it you should not have made the offer."

Fargo tensed to rush in. He must strike quickly and not give Terrell time to draw. He did not know how fast Terrell was but he must be better than most, given that Yoas and the others lived in fear of him. He only wished Terrell would turn so his back was to the tunnel.

"If only I had known that night at the lake," Bobbie Joe was saying. "But you were so handsome, and I was flattered you wanted me."

"You should be flattered," Mad Dog said.

"I was always so particular about men, too," Bobbie Joe went on as if she had not heard him. "That is the sad part. Out of all the males in the world, I picked you to be the one to take me."

"You enjoyed it. I know you enjoyed it."

"It was all right," Bobbie Joe said softly. "I didn't hear bells or a heavenly choir or any of that. But you were not as tender as I always reckoned a man would be, and after you were done you rolled off and turned your back to me instead of cuddlin' some like I wanted you to."

"You expected all that?" Mad Dog chuckled. "Hell, girl. You were a roll in the hay. Nothing more."

Bobbie Joe winced. "Yes. I see that now, too late to do me any good. But I tell you this. If I had it to do over again, I would cut off your oysters before I would let you touch me. I swear to God."

Mad Dog stood. "If that is how you feel, I will be damned if I will touch you now. Get up. I am taking you back out."

"But you agreed!" Bobbie Joe exclaimed.

"You have not lived up to your end. Instead you are talking me to death." Mad Dog's hand moved, and just like that his Colt was out and pointed at her. "On your feet."

Fargo was impressed. He has seen some slick draws. Many people considered him to be fast, but so was Terrell.

Bobbie Joe had blanched. "Do it, then. Get it over with."

Waiting for Terrell to turn was no longer an option. Fargo was poised on the balls of his feet when he heard a sound behind him, no more than a slight scrape. He started to turn but before he could he was seized by the shoulders and propelled under the stone arch with so much force, he slammed against the wall.

"What the hell?" Mad Dog blurted.

Fargo spun.

Mattox filled the opening. For someone so huge, he could be as silent as a stalking cat when he wanted to be. "I caught him listening. What do you want me to do with him?"

Mad Dog had his Colt trained on Fargo. Smirking, he answered, "Break both his arms for me so when we tie him he won't get loose again."

"Whatever you want." Tucking at the waist, Mattox entered the chamber. He had to stoop or he would hit his head. Extending his enormous arms, he flexed his fingers. "You can make this easy or you can make it hard."

"We will do hard," Fargo said. Suddenly springing, he darted aside as Mattox sought to seize him, and kicked the giant in the knee. It elicited a howl. Mattox swung a fist, but for all his strength he was ponderous and slow. Fargo ducked, bounded to one side, and kicked Mattox in the other knee.

"Damn you!" the giant roared. "Quit hopping around like a jackrabbit!"

Taking a gamble, Fargo turned his back to Mad Dog Terrell and moved so he was between them. Predictably, Mattox spread his arms wide and came at him like a runaway wagon.

A flick of Fargo's foot and a swift sidestep were all it took. He hooked Mattox's leg and the giant squawked and lost his balance and slammed into Mad Dog. Both went down. In a long bound Fargo reached Bobbie Joe. Grabbing her wrist, he flew toward the tunnel.

"Get off me, you oaf!" Mad Dog was bellowing. "I can't shoot them with you on top of me!"

Fargo let go of Bobbie Joe and ran. She did not say anything. There was no need. As fleet as deer, they wound along the tunnel until they came to where it opened into the cave mouth. The fire still crackled but no one was there. Yoas and DePue were still off up the gorge.

Fargo's luck was holding. He dashed to the horses and was reaching for a bridle when a revolver boomed and lead buzzed over his head. A glance showed Mad Dog rushing from the tunnel.

"This way!" Fargo shouted, and skirting the horses, he sprinted for all he was worth.

Bobbie Joe was breathing heavily but she kept up. "Thank you for saving me!"

"We aren't safe yet," Fargo responded.

Shouts erupted, both to their rear and up the gorge, as they raced out of the cave. A shot cracked and lead whined off the stone wall inches from Fargo's head.

Fargo had hoped that once they were around the bend the gorge would widen, or else they would find ready cover in the form of boulders. But no, the gorge narrowed, and suddenly they were running along a ledge barely wider than their feet. To the left reared the stone rampart; to their right was a hundred-foot drop.

A single misstep would send them over the edge. Fargo stared at the ledge, not at the water below or the heights above. The ledge, and only the ledge.

Another shot thundered.

"Skye!" Bobbie Joe wailed.

Fargo risked a glance back. She had not been shot. She was pointing behind her, at Mad Dog and Mattox. "Keep running!" he urged.

Another turn brought them a temporary reprieve. The ledge widened, which was encouraging. Even better, a cleft appeared in the stone wall. Wide enough for a horse, it led toward the top. Fargo did not hesitate. He hurtled up it.

"They are still after us!" Bobbie Joe shouted.

Fargo didn't doubt it. Mad Dog would not rest until

he caught them. But that would take some doing provided they could reach cover. Forest, preferably, heavy with undergrowth.

The incline grew steeper. The cleft was so narrow that in places Fargo had to squeeze through. Another thirty feet and they would reach the top.

The bright sunlight, after the gloom of the gorge, nearly blinded him. Fargo blinked and saw level ground, and beyond, welcome woodland. He started toward it.

The next moment a shot spanged below them, and Bobbie Joe Jentry cried out, "Skye! I'm hit!"

16

Fargo turned just in time to catch her. She stumbled into his arms, her face contorted in pain. Glancing down the cleft, Fargo saw Mad Dog Terrell with a smoking rifle to his shoulder. Quickly, Fargo pulled her toward the trees, shifting so he could examine her back as they ran. The slug had taken her high in the left shoulder, digging a furrow that was slowly welling up with blood. As near as he could tell, it had missed the bone and had not severed a major vein, or there would be a lot more blood. "It looks like you will live," he informed her. "I can't doctor you yet, though."

"I understand," Bobbie Joe gasped.

The forest closed around them. Fargo supported her until she could run on her own, and then run they did. She could not go as fast as before but she did well enough that they were deep into the thick timber when angry shouts warned them the outlaws had reached the top of the gorge and were giving chase.

"Go on without me," Bobbie Joe urged. "I am slowin' you down."

"We stay together," Fargo said.

"Save yourself," Bobbie Joe insisted. "They are bound to catch us if you stick with me."

"Save your breath for running." Fargo would be damned if he would leave her. He wished he had a weapon, any weapon, but that could wait. The important thing was to elude the outlaws.

For the next five minutes they grimly sped for their lives.

Now and then a shout behind them reminded them that Mad Dog and company were still after them. The shouts also gave Fargo some idea of how far back they were.

All the while, Fargo cast about for a hiding place or a means of throwing the killers off their scent. He had no doubt one or two of them could track. Yoas, most probably, maybe Mad Dog, too. But they could not track as well as he could. It was not bragging to say that few men could.

Bobbie Joe's shirt was stained dark but the bleeding had about stopped. She was pale, ungodly pale, and beads of sweat sprinkled her forehead. But she did not give up. She had grit, this one. Grit to spare.

"How are you holding up?"

"I could dance a jig."

Fargo smiled encouragement and forged on. The forest seemed to go on forever. He noted with satisfaction that the sun was almost to the western horizon. Soon night would fall, and with it, a reprieve. He had not heard any shouting in a while, which suggested the outlaws had fallen a considerable distance behind. "We will stop soon so you can rest."

"Like hell. You are not gettin' caught on my account."

"You are some woman, Bobbie Joe Jentry."

"If you are flirtin' with me, you picked a poor time. You might want to wait until I am stitched up and in the mood."

Fargo grinned.

Along about sunset the woods gave way to broken country. A draw looked promising. The sides were high enough to hide them and it was wide enough that they could lie down if they wanted. Fargo went about a hundred yards into it, then halted.

"Why did you stop?" Bobbie Joe asked. "There is plenty of light yet. We can go another mile or two."

"This will do for now." Fargo motioned for her to sit and she did so without arguing. "Take off your shirt."

"I beg your pardon."

"Don't worry. I am not in the mood at the moment, either."

Bobbie Joe hesitated, then gingerly undid the shirt and peeled it from her shoulder. She kept one arm over her bosom, which was too bad. From what Fargo could see, her breasts were as full and firm as twin melons. He gave his head a toss to shed the notion he was entertaining, and bent down.

The furrow was a quarter of an inch deep and caked with dried blood.

"You need to take your shirt all the way off so I can rip a strip from the bottom," Fargo suggested.

"Like hell," Bobbie Joe responded. "I bought this shirt with my own money. I will get by without a bandage."

"You are being pigheaded."

"It is my shoulder." Bobbie Joe ended the debate by pulling her shirt up and buttoning it. Grimacing, she sank back and closed her eyes. "I could sleep for a month."

"How about if you stay here while I go look for water and rustle us up something to eat?"

"The water would be nice but I don't think I can eat right now," Bobbie Joe said wearily.

Fargo climbed to the top of the draw and surveyed the countryside, which was shrouded in the gathering twilight. There was no sign of a stream or a lake anywhere. He roved in a circle that brought him back to the draw at the point where he had climbed out just as full night fell. Disappointed, he descended to the bottom.

"No water, I take it?" Bobbie Joe said, and licked her lips.

"None nearby. I will try again, farther this time. I might be gone an hour or two, so don't fret."

"You are not leavin' me alone. I can hold out until mornin'."

"I am a grown man. I am not scared of the dark."

"It is not you I am thinkin' of," Bobbie Joe said. "I am in no shape to fight if they find me. Besides, you could search all night and not find anything. We will look together at first light."

"Are you sure?" Fargo could imagine how thirsty she was.

Bobbie Joe nodded and patted the ground. "Please. Have a seat. Let's just rest."

Fargo reluctantly obliged her. It did feel good to get off his feet. He was bone tired and sore all over and had a few bruises from his clash with Mattox. "I need to get my hands on a gun."

"And I need wings so I can fly on home." Bobbie Joe sighed and turned so she faced him. "I sure made a mess of things, didn't I?"

Fargo shrugged. "You thought you were in love."

"I *was* in love," she amended. "And I took it for granted he loved me. When that man the deputy sent showed up at our cabin, my pa didn't want me to go. But I had to come so I could warn Mad Dog."

"You did what you thought was right."

Bobbie Joe smiled. "Why do you keep makin' excuses for me? I was a blamed fool. For the first time in my life my heart ruled my head, and look at where it got me."

"How do you feel about Terrell now?" Fargo asked to gauge how fully he could trust her.

"The son of a bitch," Bobbie Joe snapped. "Give me a six-shooter and I will show you. I will shoot him to ribbons. But before he dies, I want to take a knife to the part of him that was inside of me that night by the lake."

"You can be vicious," Fargo said, smiling.

"An eye for an eye, a tooth for a tooth. He did me wrong and I will do him the same. When I am done, he will never do another woman wrong again."

Fargo had a thought that made him sit up in surprise. "Your family. Your clan."

"What about them?"

"They are a lot closer than Springfield. Would they help if we went to them and explained?"

Bobbie Joe started to shake and for a moment Fargo thought she was in pain but then he heard her low laughter.

"What?"

"You want me to tell my folks that I let Mad Dog Terrell make love to me? If my pa found out, he would

123

take a switch to my backside and blister me raw. Ma would skin me and make me eat the skin." Bobbie Joe smiled. "I can do without that, thank you very much."

"You are a grown woman. They can't stop you from doing what you want."

"Spoken like someone who has never had kids. No matter how old I get, my folks will always be my folks, and they will always expect me to behave like a lady." Bobbie Joe closed her eyes and settled back. "I am so tired, I could sleep for a month of Sundays."

Fargo waited until her bosom was rising and falling in deep slumber, then he rose and moved to the top of the draw. Stars dotted the firmament, along with a crescent of moon. To the south a coyote yipped. Soon the dark would be alive with the shrieks of predator and prey.

A glance in the direction of the gorge revealed an orange finger of flame. The outlaws had made camp for the night.

Fargo was relieved. It meant Bobbie Joe could rest. He could use some sleep, too, but he knew if he laid down he would only toss and turn so he decided to stay up until he couldn't keep his eyes open.

A brisk breeze fanned his face. A few clouds floated overhead, pale against the ink of sky. It would be nice if it rained, obliterating their tracks, Fargo mused, but there was no chance of that.

A twig snapped off in the brush. Instantly alert, Fargo flattened. A low grunt established it was an animal. The crackle of its passage suggested a bear, but it was moving away from them, not toward them. He sat up and listened until the sounds faded.

Fargo did not like being unarmed. The only times he ever went without his Colt and the toothpick were when he took a bath or made love, and even then he always kept them close. He touched his hip where his Colt should be, and swore. Missouri was not as tame as some states back East. Bears and cougars abounded, and beasts of the human variety were all too plentiful. Mad Dog Terrell and his gang were proof of that.

Fargo missed the far-off prairie and even farther Rockies. As dangerous as they were, they were home to him. He had roamed them for so long, he could not conceive of living differently than he did. Part of it had to do with his wanderlust. There was a lot he had not seen yet.

A sound put an end to Fargo's musing, a sound he took to be a stealthy footfall. He flattened again. For the longest while he lay there, waiting for whatever made the sound to reveal itself. Nothing did. Nerves, he decided, and sat up again.

"Skye? Where are you?"

The whisper brought Fargo in a hurry to the bottom of the draw. Bobbie Joe had a hand to her shoulder. "Are you all right?"

"I can't sleep. I have tried but I keep wakin' up. It's this damn wound. It hurts and it itches."

"You should have let me go for water." Fargo sank down beside her. "In the morning it will be the first thing we do."

"Any sign of them?"

Fargo told her about the campfire. "We are safe until daylight. Once the sun is up they will come on hard and fast. We must be ready."

"There are four of them and two of us. They have guns and we don't. I would not give two bits for our chances."

"Where is your spunk? Your sand?" Fargo placed his hand on hers. "I didn't take you for the sort to give up."

"And I'm not. But you have to admit that we are in a fix," Bobbie Joe said. "We could be dead by mornin'."

A howl nipped Fargo's reply. It was so loud, and so close, that Bobbie Joe gave a start, her nails digging into his palm.

"That sounded like a wolf but they are scarce in these parts."

Fargo groped the ground for a rock he could use. Not that he thought the wolf, if indeed it was one, would prove to be a danger. Wolves rarely attacked people.

The only time he ever heard of it happening was a few years back, and then the wolf had been old and partly lame and starving to death.

When, after a while, the howl was not repeated, Bobbie Joe whispered, "I reckon it has gone away." She turned to him, her face as pale as ever. "I am sorry for slowin' you down, and for bein' such a bother."

"You were shot, remember? I would call that a good excuse. Not that you need one."

"That is not what I meant by a bother, and you know it."

"You are starting to sound like Deputy Gavin, and look where his guilt got him." Fargo was about to suggest she rest her head on his shoulder when he thought he heard the same stealthy footfall as before, this time from the top of the draw. He twisted to scan the rim but did not see anything.

"What is it?" Bobbie Joe whispered.

"Maybe nothing," Fargo said. But he had to be sure. "Wait here. If something happens to me, get to the woods and climb a tree." She would be safer from meat eaters than in the draw.

"I will not leave you."

"Damn contrary females," Fargo groused.

Bobbie Joe mustered a wan smile. "We learn it from you men. You be careful."

The slope had too much loose earth and too many small stones. Fargo tried not to make noise but felt dirt and stones slide from under him. The clatter was unnaturally loud, and he froze.

From out of the night came a faint bestial growl. The wolf, or whatever it was, was well off in the woods.

Fargo inched higher. His eyes cleared the rim and he glanced to the right and the left. Once again, nothing. Feeling slightly foolish, he climbed out of the draw, and crouched. Absolutely nothing. He did not let it bother him. It was better to err on the side of caution than to push up daisies.

In the distance the orange finger continued to glow. Fargo considered taking the fight to them, but no, he refused to leave Bobbie Joe alone. He turned to go back down, and as he did, part of the ground seemed to rise up and spring at him.

But it was not the ground; it was Yoas.

Metal glinted in the starlight as his deadly double-edged dagger arced at Fargo's neck.

17

Fargo swept his arm up, striking Yoas's arm, and the blade missed. Instantly, he sought to grab Yoas's wrist but Yoas was too quick. Again the dagger flicked out, at Fargo's belly, and only Fargo's lightning reflexes saved him. He circled to the right; Yoas circled to the left. When Yoas stopped, he stopped.

"Give up, gringo, and you live a little longer."

"Is that what your lord and master told you to say?" Fargo responded while listening for some sign of the others.

"No man is my master," Yoas spat. "I stay with Mad Dog because I want to. Because I get to do what I like best." His teeth flashed in a sneer. "I get to kill."

Fargo was almost certain Yoas was alone but he could not be completely sure, and that was worrisome. It occurred to him that Yoas might be distracting him so one of the others could jump him from behind. He must end it quickly. To that end, he feinted, then lunged. He was near enough that if he could get his hands on the smaller man's wrists, it would soon be over.

But a rattlesnake had nothing over Yoas. The man was living quicksilver. Fargo's fingers closed on thin air. To add insult to insult, Yoas snickered and said, "If that is all the quicker you are, gringo, you are as good as dead."

Yoas came at Fargo weaving a glittering tapestry of cold steel. Fargo dodged, twisted, backpedaled. He staved off death again and again, but he could not keep it up forever. He knew it and Yoas knew it. Thrusting and slashing, the deadly breed did not permit Fargo a moment's respite. Fargo had to keep moving, or die.

Their grim dance might have gone on longer had the unforeseen not reared its unexpected head.

Out of the draw came Bobbie Joe Jentry. Weak from her wound and the long chase, she moved unsteadily, as if drunk. "What is going on up here?" she demanded as she came over the top.

Yoas saw his chance. Before Fargo could warn her, Yoas caught hold of Bobbie Joe's arm and bent it behind her back while simultaneously pressing the tip of his dagger to her side. "Don't move or I kill her where she stands!"

Fargo believed him but apparently Bobbie Joe did not. Weak though she was, she drove her elbow back, catching Yoas in the face. There was the crunch of cartilage and Yoas let go of her and leaped beyond her reach, blood spurting from his broken nose. "Bitch! You rotten, stinking bitch!"

For a few seconds Yoas was focused on her, and Fargo sprang. Yoas's knife streaked to meet him but he grabbed the killer's wrist and held it while throwing a punch that clipped Yoas on the temple. Fargo had gone for the jaw but at the last split second, Yoas turned his head.

Fargo seized the breed's other wrist. Locked together, they grappled. Fargo was bigger but Yoas was no weakling, and although Fargo tried his best to trip him or throw him to the ground, Yoas nimbly countered every move.

In the dark it was inevitable that one of them would make a mistake. Fargo, in seeking to trip Yoas, flung his leg out too far and lost his balance. He teetered but would have regained his footing had the ground under him not given way. Too late, he realized he was on the edge of the draw. Gravity and loose stones conspired against him, and the next thing he knew, he was on his back.

Bobbie Joe yelled something but Fargo did not catch

what she said. He was sliding headfirst toward the bottom. Thinking quick, he dug in his elbows. But no sooner did he stop than a human wolverine arced out of the air and landed on his chest.

"Die!" Yoas shrieked, and stabbed at Fargo's heart. Fargo caught the descending arm and held it. Yoas's other hand snaked at his face, at his eyes. By jerking his head, Fargo escaped injury. Then fingers were on his throat, gouging deep, attempting to choke off his breath and do what the knife had been unable to do so far.

Struggling furiously, Fargo slammed his knee into Yoas's side. The howl of pain it brought was incentive for Fargo to do it again, and yet a third time. Yoas cried out anew and his grip slackened.

Bucking upward, Fargo sent the breed tumbling to the bottom of the draw. He sprang upright and crouched, ready for the next rush, but Yoas did not get up. The breed was stunned, Fargo thought, and bounded down to take the knife and finish it. But it was already finished, as Fargo discovered when he rolled Yoas onto his back.

Jutting from his sternum was the silver hilt. Yoas had fallen on his own blade.

"I'll be damned," Fargo said. He was suddenly so tired, he could not stand up.

More stones clattered, and Bobbie Joe knelt beside him. "You did it!" she happily exclaimed. "One down and three to go."

Fargo did not share her elation. He would celebrate when all four were dead, not before.

"Are you hurt? Did he cut you? Is there anything I can do?"

"No, no and no," Fargo answered. Wrapping his fingers around the knife, he pulled the blade out. It made a sucking sound as it came free. Blood dripped from the steel, blood he wiped off on Yoas's shirt. Then he unbuckled Yoas's gun belt, adjusted it, and strapped the belt around his own waist. He preferred a Colt but the Cooper revolver Yoas had favored would do. He checked that there were six pills in the wheel. Then, twirling it into the holster, he gave a grunt of satisfaction.

Bobbie Joe was staring at the dead outlaw. "Why didn't he just shoot you?"

"Who knows?" Fargo replied. "Maybe he wanted to use the dagger, or maybe Mad Dog told him to take me alive and he changed his mind once he saw how hard it would be." Either way, Fargo had been fortunate.

"I wish it was Mad Dog lying there," Bobbie Joe said.

"It is too bad he wasn't a two-gun man," Fargo said, holding the dagger out to her. "This will have to do until we get our hands on another revolver or a rifle."

Bobbie Joe carefully slid the blade under her belt. "When they come after us tomorrow they are in for a surprise."

"Why wait for them to come to us?" Fargo asked. "Why not end it? Now?"

"*Us* attack *them*?"

"It is the last thing they will expect." Fargo placed his hand on the Cooper. "Three shots and it is over. You wait here."

"Hold on," Bobbie Joe said, snagging his sleeve as he started to rise. "When will you get it through your thick head that we are in this together? Where you go, I go."

"You are safer here."

"I want to see them die. I want to watch Mad Dog spit up blood."

"What if I ask you real nice?" Fargo tried.

"I will tell you no, real nice." Bobbie Joe smiled sweetly. "Do we get to it or waste more time squabblin'?"

"Women," Fargo muttered, and stood. "Stay close to me. If your wound acts up, you are to let me know."

"You worry about runnin' into one of the others before we get there."

Fargo had not thought of that. Yoas might not be the only one hunting for them.

"What are you waitin' on?" Bobbie Joe asked. "If you have changed your mind, give me the pistol and I will do it myself."

"You are not long on patience, are you?"

"Not when there is revenge to be had," Bobbie Joe

131

said. "And one more thing. You can shoot the Cajun and the ox but Mad Dog is mine." She touched the silver hilt. "He will scream and scream before I am done."

Fargo believed her. Hill folk were notoriously merciless to their enemies. He headed up out of the draw. The distant finger of flame was still there. So she would not have any difficulty keeping up, he hiked toward it at a slow pace. If she caught on, she did not say anything.

They were almost to the forest when Bobbie Joe whispered, "Before I forget, I have a favor to ask."

"Another one?"

"If they should get me before I get Mad Dog, I want you to do him for me. Do him like an Apache would. Do him so when he shows up in hell, they will have to put him back together."

"That's your favor?"

Her eyes were lovely in the starlight. "I just don't want to die knowin' he won't get his."

"Whoever said females are squeamish never met you," Fargo remarked.

"I am not gentle, like women are supposed to be. I have lived in the wild all my life and I suppose I am part wild myself. When someone hurts me, I hurt them back. If you think that is wrong of me, so be it. I will not apologize for bein' me."

"I wouldn't ask you to," Fargo whispered, but she seemed not to notice.

"I am sick and tired of people judgin' me by how they think and not how I think. Out here it is do or die. Out here we can never let our enemies get the better of us, and if they do, we have to make them pay or they will think they can get the better of us any time they want."

"You do not need to explain."

"I don't?"

"You are a fine woman as you are. If I were in your boots, I would do the same."

"Really?" Bobbie Joe grinned. "When this is over, if we survive, I will make love to you until your pecker falls off."

"When this is over, if we survive, I will let you."

Bobbie Joe's teeth flashed and she leaned toward him and pecked him on the cheek.

"If that is your idea of thanks, it is a poor one," Fargo teased.

"Oh, really?"

Suddenly Bobbie Joe was pressed against him, her full lips on his, her bosom flush with his chest. Fargo responded in kind. Their kiss went on a good long while. Finally Bobbie Joe pulled back and said huskily, "You put Mad Dog to shame. Remind me to mention that to him before he breathes his last."

Fargo would have liked to kiss her some more but there was the deadly business at hand to attend to. "Keep your eyes skinned. From here on out we cannot afford a mistake."

They entered the woods. The dark was near total except where relieved by starlight filtering through breaks in the canopy. Trees, bushes, thickets, everything was distorted, a chaotic maze of shadowy shapes that confused the eye unless one was familiar with the woods at night. Fargo was, but that made the shadows no less a trial to his senses. He had to keep a tight rein on his imagination or it would have him seeing figures crouched behind every tree.

The night had gone unnaturally quiet. That in itself was a bad sign. The lesser animals only fell silent when a predator was abroad, or man.

Fargo had the Cooper out, his thumb on the hammer. It was a single-action and had to be cocked to be fired, but then, so was his Colt.

The fire was a lot brighter. They were getting close. Fargo thought he saw someone sitting close to it but he could not be certain thanks to the vegetation.

To move without making noise was a challenge. Bobbie Joe was up to it, though. When it came to woodlore, most country girls put their citified cousins to shame. She was not quite as adept as Fargo but she was good, damn good, and his admiration of her rose another notch.

The campfire was several hundred feet ahead when something moved off to the right. Fargo froze and Bobbie Joe imitated his example. As if it had seen them or sensed them, the thing stopped, too.

Fargo tried to make out what it was. He stared until his eyes were fit to pop from his head. He dared not move until he knew.

To the north another coyote yipped and was answered by one surprisingly close to the south. The thing moved, enough for Fargo to see that it walked on four legs, not two. His thumb eased a trifle.

Whatever it was, it appeared to be staring at the fire. Maybe it was curious. Or else it was a meat eater with designs on human flesh.

The minutes crawled by.

Of all the traits a frontiersman should possess, patience was arguably the most important. Whether hunting beasts or other men, patience often meant the difference between success and death. Fargo's patience paid off. The creature turned, its silhouette revealing it for what it was.

"A buck!" Bobbie Joe whispered.

Fargo did not move. Otherwise, he might spook it, and forewarn the outlaws. To occupy himself, he envisioned putting slugs into Terrell, Mattox and DePue. He would like doing that. He was not bloodthirsty by nature. He did not kill for killing's sake. But if anyone ever deserved to be planted toes up, those three did. For years they had terrorized, plundered and murdered to their hearts' content. It was high time someone put a stop to it.

Life on the frontier would never be considered truly safe until they and all those like them were exterminated.

The buck was gone.

Fargo nudged Bobbie Joe and crept on. Fifty yards from the fire he eased onto his hands and knees. Twenty yards out he sank onto his belly and crawled.

There was only one person by the fire. Whoever it was, he was bundled in a blanket, the folds up around his head so Fargo could not see his face or hair. The person was not big enough to be Mattox. It had to be either Mad Dog or the Cajun.

The clearing was small. Fargo looked for sleeping

forms but saw none. Where were the other two? he wondered. Off hunting for Bobbie Joe and him? He stopped, wary of a trap.

Bobbie Joe glanced at him and gestured for them to keep crawling but Fargo shook his head. He would wait a while and see if the other two came back. Bobbie Joe gestured again, and pulled on his shirt. When he did not move, she placed her mouth to his ear.

"What is the matter?"

"It could be a trick." Fargo was damned if he would show himself until he was confident it wasn't.

Then the figure by the fire lowered the blanket.

Bathed in the rosy glow of the fire were the pretty features of Lucille Sparks.

18

Fargo's first impulse was to rise and rush out but he stayed where he was. The outlaws had to be around somewhere and he preferred to spot them before they spotted him.

Lucille poured coffee into a tin cup and sipped. Her hair was disheveled and she had the weary aspect of someone who had not slept well in days. Stifling a yawn, she stared into the fire and pulled the blanket back up to her shoulders.

Fargo felt a light touch on his arm. Bobbie Joe was looking at him quizzically, apparently wondering why he was just lying there. He motioned at the woods. She gazed about them, then nodded to show him she understood.

More time dragged but the outlaws did not appear. Lucy went on sipping and occasionally yawning.

Fargo began to wonder how it was that Mad Dog had not killed her, and why she appeared so calm, and even more important, how she got there when he had seen no sign of her at the cave. It dawned on him that maybe he was mistaken, maybe she was there on her own, maybe she had escaped from Terrell and had been wandering the mountains ever since. Twisting so his mouth brushed Bobbie Joe's ear, he whispered, "Stay hid. I am going to talk to her."

Bobbie Joe seemed about to say something but changed her mind.

Rising, Fargo warily moved into the open. He expected

Lucy Sparks to jump to her feet or call out his name or show some excitement but all she did was glance up and tiredly smile.

"Well, look who it is."

"Where are they?" Fargo asked, scouring the benighted vegetation.

"Who?" Lucy responded.

"Mad Dog Terrell and his killers." Fargo looked at her. "Are you telling me that you are alone? That you made the fire? The coffee?"

"That I did," Lucy said. "Why don't you join me? You must forgive me if I do not get up but I am so tired I can barely keep my eyes open."

Fargo went over to her but he did not sit down. Not yet. Not until he was convinced it was safe. "I thought you were dead."

"There are times when I wish I were," Lucy said sadly. "My life has been a nightmare since I saw you last."

"I can imagine," Fargo said. "I was part of the posse that was hunting for you. Most of them are dead."

The lines in Lucy's face deepened. "I am sorry to hear that. The last thing I want is more innocent blood on my conscience." She motioned. "Please. Have a seat. I would like to hear all about it, and I would rather not get a crick in my neck from staring up at you."

Against his better judgment, Fargo obliged her. "Ladies first," he said. "The last I heard, Mad Dog and you had ridden off together and only Mad Dog came back."

"At the cabin, you mean? Yes, I had had enough. There is only so much a body can stand."

"Did he harm you?" Fargo asked. "Did he—" He did not finish the question.

"Bruce?" Lucy said, and uttered a short, brittle laugh. "Oh, no. He would never do anything like that. Not to me."

"You are no different from any other woman."

Lucy held the tin cup in both hands and stared into it, adrift in thought. At length she said, "Isn't it strange how life never turns out as we expect? When I was little I never foresaw anything like this."

"Who can predict the future?" Fargo responded.

"It is more than that," Lucy said. "We think we have it all worked out, we think we will do this or that or the other, but life comes along and knocks us off our feet and won't let us get back up again."

Fargo had no idea what she was talking about, and said so.

"I am talking about happiness. About living as we want and not as life would have us live. Take me, for example. I always wanted a husband and a family and a nice home. Is that too much to ask? I didn't think so. But life has dictated otherwise."

"You are young yet, you are good-looking," Fargo told her. "You can still have all that."

"No, I can't," Lucy insisted. "I refuse to put loved ones through hell. I refuse to have them suffer as I have suffered."

Again she was not making sense. "You need to be more clear," Fargo said.

"I am a good person. I am polite and kind to everyone I meet. I always obeyed my parents. Well, almost always. I was a normal child. I never hurt a fly if I could help it."

"There is a point to this?" If so, Fargo could not guess what it was. To him, she was rambling, perhaps as a consequence of her fatigue. He kept scouring the woods but he did not see any cause for alarm. Resting his forearms across his knees, he held the Cooper pointed at the ground.

"Bear with me," Lucy requested. She drained her coffee and set the cup down. Her hand disappeared under her blanket and then reappeared holding a revolver that she calmly trained on him and calmly cocked.

Fargo stiffened. "What is that for?"

"To shoot you with if you do not do exactly as I tell you," Lucy said with more of that unnatural calm. "Be so kind as to drop your pistol. Please, no sudden moves. I like you, Skye. I like you a lot, and I would rather not kill you if I don't have to but I will if you force me."

"Is this how you show that you like someone?" Fargo

138

snapped, but he did as she wanted. Something in her eyes warned him she would do exactly as she threatened.

"You are still alive, aren't you?" Lucy said, and smiled sweetly. "For a while, anyhow. Time enough for me to explain so you won't think ill of me."

"Too late for that."

"Now, now. Be nice." Lucy shifted so she faced him and backed away a foot or so. "Hear me out, please. You see, I wasn't an only child. I had a sibling who was forever getting into trouble. He never listened to our parents, never heeded the teacher in school, never would give an ear to the parson. He always did what he wanted when he wanted. If there is a black sheep in every family, then he is ours."

"He?" Fargo repeated, his gut tightening.

"My brother. He is a few years old than me. Even though he was always in hot water, I adored him. He never mistreated me, never did to me the things he did to others and to animals." Lucy paused. "He would torture kittens and puppies for the fun of it. Chop off their tails and stick nails through their paws. Or throw a cat and a small dog into a sack and tie the sack shut. Or cut the ears off of a little bunny."

"Hell," Fargo said.

"I suppose it was inevitable that he would tire of animals and move on to people. When he was seventeen he killed a little boy. Did things I can't talk about, they were so horrible. But someone saw him leaving the shed where he did it, and he had to flee for his life. He came west. To Missouri."

"Hell, hell, hell," Fargo amplified his sentiments.

"For a few years he tried to live like everyone else. He changed his last name and got a job. But then the old urges returned, stronger than ever, and he took to killing and robbing. In time others joined him, until now he is considered the worst outlaw in the state if not the whole country."

"Mad Dog Terrell is your brother," Fargo stated the obvious.

"Bruce Sparks is my brother. He took the name Terrell because it was the name of our parson back home. It amused him, you see, to insult the parson like that." Lucy laughed lightly. "I must admit even I find that funny."

"I never would have guessed," Fargo admitted.

"Why should you? He has never told anyone who he really is or that he was from Ohio. Most think he was born and bred right here in Missouri." Lucy was quiet a bit. "He kept in touch, though. From time to time I would get a letter. I never showed them to our parents. I couldn't. He would talk about his sprees, as he calls them. About some of the people he has killed and how he killed them."

"That is some brother you have."

Lucy bit her lower lip. "I know, I know. But he *is* my brother and I care for him. Which is why I came to Springfield. I was hoping I could convince him to give up his wild ways and come back to Ohio. But he refused to listen. So I decided to go back alone."

"He didn't want you to leave," Fargo guessed.

"No, he didn't. He stopped the stage and took me off. We went to the cabin with his men and then he and I went off up into the hills to talk things over in private. It didn't do any good. He still refuses to walk the straight and narrow."

"You are beating your head against a tree."

"I know that now," Lucy said. "But I can't very well turn my back on him, can I? I mean, if he needs help, I have to help him, don't I? It is what sisters do for their brothers."

Fargo knew what was coming and wanted to beat his own head against a tree for being so stupid.

"Bruce asked me to be the bait. I didn't want to, but he told me that if you and the girl get away, more men will come to try and kill him, and I can't have that." Lucy held up her other hand. "Before you say anything, yes, he has brought this down on his own head. But as I keep saying—"

"He is your brother," Fargo finished for her.

"Exactly." Lucy brightened, then raised her voice and called out, "How did I do, Bruce?"

Out of the dark they came, Mad Dog and Mattox and DePue. The latter was pushing Bobbie Joe ahead of him, the knife Fargo had given her now in the Cajun's possession.

"You did right fine, sis," Mad Dog said. "And look at who we found trying to sneak up on you with a pig-sticker." He shoved Bobbie Joe, causing her to stumble and fall to her knees.

Both Mattox and DePue had their revolvers out. Both covered Fargo as Mad Dog walked up to him and without any warning whatsoever slugged Fargo in the gut.

The pain was awful. Doubling over, Fargo held his arms over his stomach to ward off another blow, should it come. But Mad Dog merely chuckled. "What was that for?" Fargo spat out.

"I don't really need a reason," Mad Dog said. "But if you do, how about for the aggravation you have caused me?"

"Ask him about Yoas," Mattox said.

Mad Dog sniffed. "Yes, where is our nasty little breed? I sent him to have a look around and he never came back."

"His days of doing anything are done," Fargo said.

"In other words, he is dead." Mad Dog sighed. "That is too bad. Replacing him will take some doing. Men who like to slit throats as much as I do are hard to find."

Bobbie Joe snorted. "You call yourselves men? Scum is more like it. Vermin the world will be better off without."

"Did I say you could talk?" Mad Dog asked, and back-handed her across the face, knocking her on her side. Drawing back his leg, he taunted, "How about if I kick your teeth in?"

"No!" Lucy Sparks cried. "Please, Bruce. You promised to go easy on them, at least until I leave."

Hissing between his clenched teeth, Mad Dog set his foot down. "That I did, but I can't say I like it much." He barked for Mattox to bind them, then turned back to his sister. "You are the only person in this whole world who can make me do something I do not want to."

"I am grateful," Lucy said. "No matter what else you have done, you have always been a good brother."

Fargo was astounded when Mad Dog's eyes moistened. He would have sworn the killer did not have a shred of feeling for anyone.

Evidently he was not the only one who was surprised. "Are you all right, *mon ami*?" DePue wondered. "I have never seen you act like this."

"I'm fine!" Mad Dog snarled with an angry toss of his head. "Why are you looking at me when you are supposed to be looking at them?"

"Sorry," DePue said quickly.

Mattox had produced a length of rope and now wagged it at Fargo. "Turn around so I can get this done."

Fargo had made up his mind he was not going to allow them to bind him again. He had been lucky to escape the first time. He was pushing that luck to think he could do it a second time. As he started to turn he glanced down at Bobbie Joe and gave a barely perceptible nod. Clever girl that she was, she immediately understood, and winked.

"Put your arms behind you," Mattox instructed.

"Whatever you say," Fargo responded, and spun, his right foot rising in an arc that ended where it would hurt any man the most. He shoved Mattox toward DePue. A bound brought him to Lucy, and before she could think to resist, he had wrenched the revolver from her grasp and jammed the muzzle against her temple while pivoting behind her.

Mad Dog had whipped out his own six-gun but now he froze. "No!" he shouted as DePue and Mattox leveled theirs. "You might hit my sister!"

Lucy went to take a step but Fargo looped his other arm around her waist. "Stay right where you are." Careful not to expose more of himself than he could avoid, he said over her shoulder, "Drop your guns, all of you."

"No," Mad Dog said.

"I will shoot her if you don't," Fargo bluffed. He could

142

no more gun down an unarmed woman than he could a child.

"No, you won't," Mad Dog responded.

"Bruce?" Lucy said uncertainly.

"Don't you worry, sis. We have us a standoff. He won't shoot you because if he does we will empty our six-guns into him." Mad Dog gestured at Mattox and DePue and they began to sidle to the right and the left, respectively.

"Stay where you are," Fargo commanded. He had to get out of there while he still could. "Bobbie Joe, get over here by me." To Mad Dog he said, "We are leaving and we are taking your sister with us."

"Like hell you are," Mad Dog replied. The click of his pearl-handled Colt's hammer was ominously loud.

19

Was Mad Dog Terrell as mad as everyone claimed? Or was there a shred of sanity behind those uncanny, unnerving eyes? "She is your sister," Fargo appealed to whatever shred was left. "If you want her dead, squeeze the trigger."

"Bruce, please," Lucy pleaded.

Mad Dog—or Bruce Sparks—vented a low growl, much as an animal would, then slowly lowered his Colt. "For you, sis, and only for you. Just this once."

Fargo seized the moment. He backed away, pulling Lucy after him, Bobbie Joe at his side. Mattox and DePue glanced at one another. The pair did not like the idea of letting them get away. Both looked at Mad Dog but neither had the courage to say anything.

A few more yards and the woods closed around them. Fargo turned Lucy around and gave her a push in the direction of the gorge. "Run," he said.

"In the dark? I might trip and hurt myself."

Fargo gave her a harder push. "*Run*, damn it!" he goaded, and earned a grin from Bobbie Joe.

They ran. In the dark they did trip and stumble, Lucy a lot of times, Bobbie Joe a couple, Fargo only once. They were running flat out, or as close to it as they could, Fargo's intention to reach the cleft well ahead of their pursuers. Then it would be on to the cave, and the horses.

The horses. Fargo would take every last one, stranding the outlaws. He would personally lead the posse that came after them, personally see to it that Mad Dog and his fellow killers had done their last killing.

It was difficult to gauge distance. Fargo thought they still had a ways to go when they emerged from the undergrowth. The cleft should be straight ahead but it wasn't. They had come out south of it, at the very lip of the gorge. Wind buffeted them as they gazed into the Stygian depths.

"What now?" Lucy sarcastically asked. "Do you want me to jump?"

"I could shove you over," Bobbie Joe offered.

Fargo did the honors, but he shoved Lucy toward the cleft, not over the edge. When they reached the gap he took the lead. Lucy was next. Bobbie Joe brought up the rear.

A cold mist filled the bottom of the gorge. Fargo turned right and slowed to a cautious walk. A misstep here would pitch them into the boulder-strewn rapids. He made it safely around the bend. The mouth of the cave had to be near but it was black as pitch and he had started past it when he sensed it was there. Reaching back, he grabbed Lucy and pulled her after him.

A shot boomed from out of the cave, sounding like a cannon, and a muzzle flash stabbed the dark.

Fargo let go of Lucy and dived flat, scraping his elbows and knees. He was stunned. He could not figure out how the outlaws got there ahead of them. There had to be another way down from the top, a way only the outlaws knew. He extended the revolver but he did not shoot. He did not see anyone *to* shoot. Just the pitch black.

Neither Bobbie Joe nor Lucy had cried out. Fargo assumed they had not been hit. He heard one of them crawl toward him and whispered gruffly, "Stay still!"

"It's me," Bobbie Joe whispered back. "What do we do? We can't let them pin us here until daylight or we are as good as dead."

She was not telling Fargo anything he did not already know. Somehow they must deal with the shooter and the other two, wherever they were. "Stay here with Lucy," he whispered, and started to crawl into the cave.

"Where is she?" Bobbie Joe asked.

"Lucy?" Fargo whispered, and did not receive a reply. He groped about but she was not anywhere near him. "Damn. Where did she get to?"

At that juncture a laugh issued from the rear of the cave, but not the maniacal laugh of Mad Dog Terrell or the booming laugh of Mattox or the sly laugh of DePue. This was a raspy laugh, a mocking laugh, followed by, "What's all that jabbering out there, you sons of bitches! I can hear you whispering. But it won't do you any good. This old goat is out to end your days!"

Incredulous, Fargo rose onto his elbows. "Old Charley? Is that you?"

"Fargo?"

"And Bobbie Joe," Fargo said, rising. "We thought you were dead, killed back at the cabin."

The old frontiersman cackled. "I thought you were Mad Dog's bunch!"

Bobbie Joe was not all that amused. "You could have shot us, you old buzzard."

"Hell, girl. It would have taken a heap of luck. I was shooting at the sound of your footsteps."

By then they had found one another. Old Charley clasped Fargo's hand and pumped it, then impulsively threw his arms around Bobbie Joe and hugged her.

"Tarnation, it makes this old coon glad to see you again! I had given you both up for dead." Old Charley paused. "You should have seen that deputy and those others. Shot to pieces, all three of them."

"How is it you are alive?" Fargo asked.

"Providence," Old Charley said. "I was clipped in the shoulder and fell from my horse and the damned critter ran off. Right away I started crawling toward the trees and made it before the outlaws could find me. They didn't look very hard. Must have figured I was a goner."

"You trailed them here on foot?" Fargo marveled.

"They weren't in any great hurry, so it was easy," Old Charley said. "I got here just as night fell and decided to stick around and surprise them when they showed up.

I reckon I should have skedaddled when I drove off the horses, but I never did have a lick of sense."

An icy finger ran down Fargo's spine. "You did what?"

"I ran off all the horses so Mad Dog is stranded afoot," Old Charley said proudly. "Mighty smart of me, don't you think?"

"Smart like a tree stump," Bobbie Joe said.

"What do you mean, girl?"

"She means we are stranded afoot, too," Fargo clarified, "and the outlaws will be here before too long."

"Let them come," Old Charley said. "There are three of us and four of them. Not bad odds, I say."

"They are better than you think," Bobbie Joe commented. "Yoas is dead."

"You don't say?" Old Charley liked to cackle. "Good riddance! Now we do the rest like you did him and the people of Missouri can breathe easy." He clapped Fargo on the arm. "I say we wait for them like I waited for you and give them the surprise of their lives."

"You missed us, remember?" Fargo noted. They must not leave anything to chance. Either they ended it once and for all, or their own lives were forfeit.

"A fire," Bobbie Joe proposed. "Near the openin'. Then we stay at the back, and when they come into the light, we drop the buzzards."

"I like that," Old Charley said.

Fargo did, too, especially since he could not think of a craftier way. He kindled the fire himself, and as the glow spread, he set eyes on the provisions stacked along the wall. Inspiration struck. With Bobbie Joe and Old Charley helping, they carried sacks of potatoes and flour, spare blankets and several saddles and other items to the bend in the gorge wall. There they stacked them on the ledge, and stepped back.

"I don't quite savvy," Old Charley said. "What good will this do? As barricades go, it is downright puny."

"They will make noise moving it," Fargo answered. "We will be keeping watch, and we are bound to hear."

"You sure are a sneaky varmint," the old frontiersman complimented him. "I will take the first watch if you want."

Fargo let him. He had something to do, something he had put off so they could erect the barrier. Now, taking a burning brand, he bent his steps into the cave and along the tunnel to the nooks that served the outlaws as living quarters. Since none of the outlaws had Fargo's Henry or his Colt, his weapons had to be there somewhere. He came to the chamber where Bobbie Joe and Mad Dog had been earlier. A quick glance disappointed him. Then he noticed bulges under the blankets, and lifting them, he grinned.

Bobbie Joe had followed him. Fargo handed her the revolver he had taken from Lucy Sparks and strapped on his own gun belt and Colt. The Arkansas toothpick he slid into its ankle sheath. He worked the Henry's lever, confirming the rifle was loaded, and with renewed confidence started back along the tunnel.

"What is your hurry?"

Fargo stopped and looked at her. Her expression was an invite, if ever there was one. "You have to be joking."

"Why?" Bobbie Joe playfully plucked at his buckskin shirt. "I like you. You like me. It could be an hour yet before Mad Dog and the others show up."

"It could be any minute," Fargo noted. It would not do to leave Old Charley to confront them alone.

"You are turnin' me down?" Bobbie Joe blinked. "I am plumb amazed."

"I am sort of amazed, myself," Fargo confessed. He could count the number of times he had declined a lady's favors on one hand and have fingers left over.

Bobbie Joe tugged on a whang. "Later, then, when this is over."

"That would suit me fine," Fargo said. He could use a week in Springfield to recuperate. With her as company, his stay would be that much more pleasant.

"I am sorry I helped get you into this mess," Bobbie Joe said. "I honestly thought I was in love."

"We have been through that already." Fargo turned to go but again she snatched at his sleeve. "What now?"

"In case one of us doesn't make it," Bobbie Joe said, and melted against him, her mouth hungrily seeking his, her tongue a velvet harbinger of her passion.

Fargo became lost in the kiss, in the feel of her warm, lush body, in the stirring below his belt. After a bit he reluctantly pried her off, saying huskily, "Save that for after, remember?"

"You can count on it."

The cave mouth was quiet save for the crackling of the fire. Old Charley was over by the opening, peering toward the bend. He heard them come out of the tunnel and smiled.

"No sign of them yet."

"It is a shame that deputy had to die," Bobbie Joe commented out of the blue. "For a law dog he wasn't half bad."

Fargo hunkered to put coffee on to brew. It would help keep them awake. He was surprised it was taking Mad Dog so long to catch up, and wondered if possibly the outlaws were waiting for dawn to break. He mentioned it to Bobbie Joe.

"Could be you are right. That handsome bastard is nothin' if not unpredictable."

"You almost sound like you still care for him," Fargo remarked, hoping that was not the case.

"Not on your life," Bobbie Joe bitterly responded. "I learned at an early age not to stick my hand in a fire twice. Before, I used to daydream of him and me together. Now I dream of emptyin' this pistol into his miserable hide." She squatted across the fire. "But don't you worry. I will share it with you."

"Share what?" Fargo idly asked while filling the pot with water.

"The reward."

Fargo looked up.

"Didn't you know? There is three thousand dollars on Mad Dog's head. Not that anyone has ever been all that anxious to collect. A few of my kin talked about tryin' that time at the lake but I talked them out of it." Bobbie Joe sighed. "If I only knew then what I know now."

The money made no difference to Fargo.

"To me it does. It has been in the back of my mind all along," Bobbie Joe confessed. "Three thousand dollars is more than anyone in my family has ever had. Hell, it is more than all of us have had, put together. I could buy me some nice things. A dress, maybe, for wearin' to town, and some dishes for my ma, and a new rifle for my pa."

"Don't get to thinking of the money when it comes time to shoot," Fargo cautioned.

"Oh, don't worry. I am not a simpleton like Mattox. I do not put the cart before the horse."

Fargo hoped not. Vengeance was one thing, greed another. It made people careless, and careless made them dead.

"What is the most money you have ever had?" Bobbie Joe asked.

Fargo had to think about it. "Close to fifty thousand dollars once," he recollected. "In a high-stakes poker game."

"Good Lord! What did you do with it?"

"I lost every cent on the very next hand."

"How could you throw that much money away?" Bobbie Joe marveled. "To me it is a fortune."

"I thought my full house would win me another fifty thousand," Fargo related. "But the other gent had four of a kind."

"You should have quit while you were ahead."

Fargo grinned. If it were that easy, he would have been rich long ago. "Sit in on a few games and then you can talk."

Bobbie Joe lapsed into silence. But it did not last long. "I wonder where that bitch got to."

"She isn't much better off than we are," Fargo observed. But he had been wondering the same thing, himself.

"If you ask me, she snuck back to her brother. She is

on his side in this, and she will do whatever she can to see us dead."

Fargo hated to admit it but Bobbie Joe might be right. For all of Lucy's insistence on doing what was right, her love for her brother had proven thicker than her morals. "I will go stand watch so Old Charley can rest," he proposed, and rose to do so.

That was when a rifle boomed out in the gorge.

20

Fargo saw the grisly result. He was looking at Old Charley when the rifle boomed, and he saw the old frontiersman jerk to the impact of a heavy caliber slug even as part of Charley's forehead exploded, spattering the cave wall with gore. The old man died never knowing what killed him, the lifeless husk oozing to the cave floor and twitching before becoming still.

Fargo ran toward the cave mouth. The shot had come from the direction they had entered the gorge, not from the direction of the bend and the cleft. But that couldn't be, unless, as he now suspected, there was another way down.

Fargo poked his head out for a quick look-see. Almost instantly a rifle spanged and lead whined off the rock inches from his face, stinging his cheek with slivers.

"I almost had you, *mon ami*! You did not lean out as far as the old man. Do so, and I will try to do better."

The Cajun. Fargo gazed at the crumpled figure, and frowned.

Bobbie Joe sidled up, armed with the revolver. "How did DePue get down there without the old man spottin' him?"

Fargo shared his idea that there was more than one route down from the top of the gorge. "Go over and watch the other side. But put out the fire first." It was the light from the campfire that had made a perfect target of Old Charley. Ironically, the very light they had counted on to enable them to pick off the outlaws.

Nodding, the hill girl hurried off.

Fargo faced the opening and cupped a hand to his mouth. "Where are your pards, DePue? Did Mad Dog and Mattox run off and leave you?"

From up the gorge, from the bend where the supplies were stacked, came a rumbling laugh. "We are not yellow, mister! We stick by our friends! As you and that girl will soon find out."

So there it was, Fargo reflected. They were boxed in. DePue to one side, Mattox to the other. Mad Dog and Lucy were unaccounted for but they were likely nearby. He decided to find out exactly where. "Let me talk to your boss," he hollered.

Silence greeted the request, until Mattox broke it with, "He is busy at the moment. But in about ten minutes you can do all the talking to him you want."

As if that were a joke of some kind, DePue laughed merrily.

Fargo swore. They were up to something. But what? He inched to the edge and risked another peek, exposing one eye. No shots rang out. He glimpsed a form crouched beside a boulder, but he did not have a clear shot.

The light in the cave was extinguished as Bobbie Joe doused the fire with the contents of the coffeepot. Smoke swirled, spreading rapidly and filling the air with its acrid scent and the odor of the coffee grounds.

An inky veil claimed the gorge.

DePue loved to hear himself talk. "That won't help you, *sot*. You are ours to kill as we please!"

The devil of it was, Fargo could tell the Cajun believed it was true. He whispered across the cave mouth to Bobbie Joe. "If you hear anything, anything at all, let me know."

"It is quiet over here," she responded. "Too quiet, to my likin'."

Fargo leaned against the wall. All they could do now was wait. He figured they would be safe until daybreak. Whatever Mad Dog had in mind, the outlaws would need light to see by.

Then DePue started up again. "Why so silent, *mon*

153

ami? Can it be you know the end that awaits you? Mad Dog is most mad. You have gotten the better of him, and no one has ever done that before. But do not flatter yourself that you will have the better of him much longer. He has plans for you. It might be better if you were to put a gun to your mouth and blow your brains out. You will suffer a lot less, eh?"

Fargo did not respond.

"Come on, talk to DePue. What harm can it do? I am not going anywhere, and neither are you."

Unexpectedly, Mattox chimed in from near the bend. "That's right. What harm can a little talking do? How about you, girl? Nothing to say?"

"Go to hell," Bobbie Joe yelled.

The gorge echoed to their sadistic glee. Both outlaws laughed long and loud. Much too long and much too loud, Fargo thought, and suddenly he snapped upright, every sense alert. They were doing it on purpose, DePue and Mattox. They were making as much noise as they could, and there could only be one reason.

Fargo spun toward the rear of the cave. Crouching, he crept along the wall. It had dawned on him that there might be a way of reaching the tunnel from above. He had never been to the end of the tunnel, only as far as the nook where he found his weapons.

DePue would not shut up. "Are you listening, girl? After Mad Dog is done with you, he is giving you to Mattox and me. He and I drew lots and I get you first. We will have a great time together, *ma chère*. I promise you."

"You can go to hell, too!" Bobbie Joe retorted.

"Not before I have savored your fine body," DePue shouted. "I will do things to you that no one has ever done. The French are great lovers, and half my blood is French."

"The other half must be that brown stuff that oozes out your ears and mouth," Bobbie Joe rejoined.

Fargo was near the tunnel. He could barely make it out, a patch of ink framed by the slightly lighter ink of the cave wall. He was about to enter it when from somewhere *above* the cave there came a yell.

"Now! Do it now!"

It sounded like Lucy Sparks. Fargo shifted toward the cave mouth just as rifles thundered in the gorge. Bobbie Joe's revolver answered them. He started to run to her aid when boots scuffed to his rear. Too late, he realized he had been right about the tunnel. Out of it hurtled a two-legged battering ram. A shoulder caught him low across the back and he was smashed flat, the Henry pinned under his chest. A knee gouged between his shoulder blades. Before he could throw his attacker off, a gun muzzle was jammed against the nape of his neck.

"One twitch and you are dead," Mad Dog Terrell warned.

From the front of the cave came a shout from Mattox. "Her six-shooter is empty! Rush her before she can reload!"

Feet pounded, Bobbie Joe swore, and a brief commotion ended with DePue exclaiming, "We have done it, my friend! We have her!"

"Get the fire going!" Mad Dog ordered. "Then yell up to my sister that she can come down." He did not move until the cave filled with light. Then he slowly raised his knee and stepped to one side, his revolver rock steady in his hand. "Turn over but don't touch your hardware."

Fargo rolled onto his back. His disgust with himself at being caught flat-footed was not helped by Terrell's smirk.

"I figured you didn't know there is a back way into the cave, or that I could get around down here blindfolded if I had to. But I never expected it to be this easy."

"Rub salt in the wound," Fargo said.

Mad Dog laughed his eerie laugh. "Here comes your friend. The question now is whether to kill you outright or do you nice and slow."

Bobbie Joe was being propelled by Mattox who had her left arm bent behind her back. He was smiling; she was scowling in fury. A bruise on her chin and another above her left eye testified to the struggle she had put up.

"This one sure is a wildcat," Mattox declared. "She tried to scratch my eyes out." Bloody lines on one cheek showed she had almost done it.

"Have her take a seat," Mad Dog said.

Without warning Mattox hooked a boot around Bobbie Joe's ankle and flung her to the cave floor. She winced as she hit, then rolled onto her side and glared up at him.

"I will kill you before this is done."

"Sure you will," Mattox responded, chuckling. "If you can do it from the grave."

"Ignore her and relieve Fargo of his artillery," Mad Dog instructed.

The giant dutifully picked up the Henry and snatched the Colt from Fargo's holster and stepped back. "Can I have this rifle of his after we are done with them? It's awful shiny," he said, admiring the brass receiver.

Fargo waited for Mad Dog to remind Mattox about the Arkansas toothpick but both appeared to have forgotten it.

Just then DePue joined them, his thumbs hooked in his gun belt. "Your sister is on her way down."

"Good." Mad Dog visibly relaxed. To Fargo he said, "All the trouble you went to, huh? What did it get you except right back where you started?"

Fargo did not answer.

"It got Yoas dead," Bobbie Joe said. "If not for your stinkin' sister, it would have gotten you dead, too."

Mad Dog never changed expression. He was smiling, and he went on smiling as he stepped over to her and brutally struck her across the head with the barrel of his revolver. Blood spurted, and she groaned and slumped. He drew back the revolver to strike her again, but didn't. Instead he snarled, "For that I will do you first."

Fargo slowly sat up. He half expected one of the outlaws to shove him back down but they didn't. Placing his arms over his knees so his hands dangled close to his ankles, he asked, "What happens to your sister when the rest of the world finds out she is related to you?"

Mad Dog tore his fierce gaze from Bobbie Joe. "The only two who know are you and this bitch, and pretty soon neither of you will be in any shape to tell anyone."

"People are bound to find out eventually," Fargo persisted. "They will hate her because of what you have done."

"Why are you bringing this up?" Mad Dog barked.

"That is what I would like to know," said Lucy Sparks, walking out of the tunnel with a torch held over her head. "What do you care what people think of me?"

Fargo shifted toward her, his right arm sliding down his leg. He made it seem perfectly natural so none of them would suspect. "I used to care. But after tonight you can't claim to be innocent. You helped them. Twice."

"I told you," Lucy said curtly. "He is my brother and I will not let any harm come to him."

"Even if it means he harms a lot of others?" Fargo said in disgust. "All the lives he takes will be on your head."

Mad Dog's face twitched in anger. "Quit talking to her like that. She is the one person in this world who cares for me."

"I care for you," Mattox said.

Fargo could feel the slight bulge of the ankle sheath under his pants. He slid his fingertips lower. "Is that how she excuses your bloodletting, Bruce? When you think about it, she is no better than you are. Scum, Bobbie Joe called you, and scum you are. You and your sister, both."

Mad Dog trembled from head to foot and his mouth worked but no sounds came out. But he did not do what Fargo wanted him to do, so Fargo gave him more cause.

"And to think, I was going to sleep with her. Thank God I didn't. If she spread her legs for me now, I would spit on them."

A piercing howl of rage burst from the throat of Mad Dog Terrell. Incensed, he leaped at Fargo and raised his

157

revolver to do to Fargo as he had done to Bobbie Joe. But in leaping, he came between Fargo and the other two outlaws.

It could not have worked out better. Fargo surged upright, his hand sweeping up and out, and the firelight gleamed on the cold steel of his toothpick. By rights he should have sheared it into Mad Dog's chest. But Lucy cried, "No!" and, springing, grabbed his wrist just as Mad Dog brought his revolver smashing down. The blow intended for Fargo's head caught her on the head, instead, and she crumpled like so much paper.

Fargo sidestepped to stab Terrell but Mad Dog dropped next to his sister, wailing, "Lucy!"

Mattox stood flat-footed, gaping in surprise.

But DePue was going for his pistol. Fargo lunged, sinking the double-edged blade to the hilt in the Cajun's throat, and then sliced from side to side. The jugular was severed. Blood sprayed as Fargo spun to confront Mattox. The giant had recovered his wits, and dropping the Henry and the Colt, spread his arms wide to catch Fargo in a bear hug.

Fargo stabbed him. The toothpick glanced off a rib and had no more effect than a real toothpick would, except that Mattox roared with rage and swung a giant fist at Fargo's face. Fargo ducked, twisted, and stabbed Mattox again, in the gut this time. Again, Mattox did not seem to notice. Backpedaling, Fargo managed a couple of steps when Mattox was on him. Those gigantic arms of his wrapped tight around Fargo's torso and Fargo was bodily lifted from the floor.

"I will snap your spine!" Mattox bellowed, pink spittle flecking his lips.

Fargo's arms were pinned but he could still move his forearms. He did the only thing he could; he stabbed the giant in the groin, not once but several times.

Mattox felt *that*. He screeched and let go and staggered, staring down at a spreading dark stain. Cupping himself, he fell to his knees, which put his throat within easy reach. A single swipe of the razor-sharp blade, and Mattox's throat was the same as DePue's.

Fargo whirled.

Mad Dog was cradling his sister's head in his lap. He looked up, saw the others were down, and jerked his revolver, roaring, "Die! Die! Die!"

In a blur Fargo lanced the toothpick into Terrell's right eye, thrusting it into the socket as far as it would go.

Mad Dog arched his back and opened his mouth, and broke out in convulsions. His revolver went off, the muzzle inches from his sister's face. Gradually his quaking subsided and he slumped over her body, a red ring spreading from under them.

Fargo scooped up his Colt but it was not needed. Mattox and DePue lay in spreading pools of their own.

Bobbie Joe moaned.

Kneeling beside her, Fargo examined her wound. She had a nasty gash but she would heal. He touched her cheek, and her eyes opened and found his.

"Are they—?"

Fargo nodded.

"Damn. You didn't let me kill any. I reckon the reward is all yours."

"We will split it," Fargo offered.

A lopsided smile curled Bobbie Joe's lips. "As soon as my head stops hurtin', how about if you and me get better acquainted? Or are you goin' to turn me down a second time?"

Fargo glanced at Mad Dog Terrell, and grinned. "I'm not that crazy."

LOOKING FORWARD!
The following is the opening
section from the next novel in the exciting
***Trailsman* series from Signet:**

The TRAILSMAN: #316
BEYOND SQUAW CREEK

Dakota Territory, 1860—where wolves prowl in
high grasses, and death hides just beyond the
horizon.

"I bet you could do a lot of damage with that thing—
couldn't you, Mr. Fargo?" the major's daughter asked.

Skye Fargo ran his lake blue eyes across the girl's willowy frame, the proud breasts pushing up from the shirtwaist of her traveling dress—pale and lightly freckled
and sheathing a small jade cameo, the same green of her
eyes, hanging by a gold chain. Her shirtwaists had been
getting tighter and tighter over the past few days since
the party had left Fort Mandan, exposing more and more
of her cleavage.

The stagecoach was parked in a canyon of White-Tail
Creek, in western Dakota Territory. Valeria Howard sat
in a canvas chair before the stage's left front wheel, holding a parasol over her regal head of bright red hair. Fargo
sat on the ground ten feet away from her, his back to a

boulder, sharpening his Arkansas toothpick on the whetstone perched on his thigh.

The soldiers escorting the stage from Fort Mandan had taken their own mounts and the stage's four-horse hitch down to the creek for water.

"Miss Howard, you got no idea," Fargo said.

Her nose wrinkled and her jade eyes glinted snootily as she continued staring at the knife on his thigh. "A rather uncouth customer, aren't you?"

"Wanna see?"

"Do I want to see *what*?"

"How much damage I can do with this thing."

Fargo followed her smoky gaze to his lap then glanced up at her, curling his upper lip. "The knife *is* the . . . uh . . . *thing* we're talking about, isn't it, Miss Howard?"

Her eyes snapped up, and a flush rose in her cream cheeks. She opened her mouth to speak but only gasped when Fargo snapped up the toothpick suddenly, and sent the six inches of razor-edged, bone-handled steel careening through the air in front of her.

She recoiled as the knife whistled past her, missing the sleeve of her muslin blouse by a half inch, to cleave the gap between two wheel spokes and bury itself, hilt deep, in one of the two brown eyes staring out from behind the hub. The Indian made a gagging sound as his head snapped back, lower jaw dropping, the remaining eye wide open.

As the girl fell over in her chair, her feathered, lemon yellow hat tumbling off her shoulder, Fargo bounded onto his knees and clawed his Colt .44 from his holster. He aimed quickly at one of the two Indians bounding onto the stage's roof from the other side, and fired.

The bullet plunked through the medicine pouch dangling from the neck of the brave standing near the driver's box. As the brave screamed and pitched backward off the coach, throwing his bow and arrow over his head, the second brave leaped forward atop a steamer trunk, gave a savage war cry, and loosed an arrow.

The feathered missile shaved a couple of whiskers from Fargo's right cheek as it whistled past his ear to clatter against the sandstone scarp behind him.

Fargo triggered the Colt twice, the slugs hammering into the brave's neck and breastbone, pinwheeling him off the coach in twin streams of geysering blood.

"Stay down!" Fargo hurdled Valeria Howard cowering on the ground beside her overturned chair, and climbed the stage to the driver's box.

Holding the cocked Colt in his right hand, he leaped onto the wooden seat and from the seat to the sandstone wall on the other side of the stage, his boots finding a narrow ledge while his left hand reached for a gnarled cedar.

As he looked up and right, a brave peered down at him from behind a thumb of rock, his face streaked with yellow and ocher war designs, eyes wide with rage. The brave raised a feathered war lance but before he could cock his throwing arm, Fargo drilled a round through his forehead, blowing him back off the scarp with a grunt, the lance clattering down the rocks behind him.

Clinging to the gnarled cedar, the .44 smoking in his right hand, the man known as the Trailsman turned to peer south through a break in the opposite canyon wall.

Since just after he'd cleaved the first buck's head with his Arkansas toothpick, he'd heard sporadic gunfire and war whoops from the direction of the creek. Through the cottonwoods lining the stream, he spied smoke puffs, prancing horses and soldiers scrambling to repel the Indians attacking from the creek's far side. Several of the savages rode horses and triggered pistols and repeating rifles while others, running afoot, loosed arrows and heaved war lances.

The soldiers returned fire while trying to hold the reins of their frightened bays.

As Fargo watched, several soldiers and cavalry mounts went down screaming, and the Indians continued charging, whooping and shooting. Only nine soldiers had been assigned to the stagecoach carrying not only the beautiful daughter of Major Howard, the commander of Fort Clark, but two army surveyors detailed to Fort Clark to plot the site of a planned sister fort near the mouth of the Wolf Head River.

Seven soldiers and the two surveyors had gone down to the creek to water the horses while, as per Fargo's orders, two privates kept watch from the butte tops. It appeared now, as two more soldiers were shot from their mounts and an Indian knelt beside a wounded surveyor, wielding a knife with which he no doubt intended to relieve the man of his hair, that none were coming back.

A spine-jellying scream rose from below. Fargo looked into the canyon. A brave stood over Valeria Howard, leaning down to smash the back of his right hand across the girl's face with a resounding smack. He pulled her up brusquely and, using both hands, ripped her shirtwaist down the front, then threw his head back to loose a delighted whoop toward the sky.

Fargo raised the .44, but he couldn't see clearly over the stage roof.

He holstered the Colt and scrambled back along the rock wall. Dropping onto the stage, he raked the .44 from its holster. Off the coach's south side, the Indian had crouched to fling the major's daughter over his back like a sack of parched corn.

Naked to her waist, the blouse hanging in tatters around her thighs, the girl kicked, screamed and pounded her fist into the brave's broad back. As the Indian turned to run off with his prize, Fargo steadied the pistol, angling it down from his right shoulder, and squeezed the trigger.

The Colt roared and leaped in his hand. The bullet ripped through the back of the Indian's head and careened out his forehead with a small geyser of bone, brains and blood.

Valeria screamed as though she herself had been shot. The Indian ran several more feet toward the gap in the canyon wall, knees bending as the life drained out of him. He fell in a rolling, tumbling heap, the girl rolling through the dust and sage ahead of him, skirts and torn shirtwaist flopping around her hips.

She'd barely stopped rolling when Fargo, having leaped down from the stage and sprinted past the quivering Indian, pulled her brusquely to her feet, her breasts jiggling, red hair falling across her face and dusty, porcelain shoulders.

"Noooo!" she cried, shaking her head wildly and beating her fists against his shoulders.

"Keep your pants on—it's me!" he yelled as he wrapped his left arm around her waist and half dragged, half carried her toward his Ovaro stallion tied behind the stagecoach.

In the south, the Indians' whoops and shouts grew louder, hooves thumping, guns popping. Evidently, a couple of soldiers were putting up a fight, but they couldn't keep it up for long. He'd seen close to twenty braves along the creek, and judging by the sound of approaching horses, they were headed toward the coach.

"Where . . . what . . . ?" the girl gasped as Fargo holstered his Colt, wrapped his hands around her waist, and tossed her onto the pinto's back. The horse was skitter-stepping at the gunfire, twitching its ears and snorting.

Fargo ripped the reins from the stage's luggage boot, then shucked his Henry repeater from the sheath attached to the saddle. "We're gonna haul ass outta here!" He swung up behind the girl. She halfheartedly crossed her arms over her breasts and looked around, sobbing.

As the Trailsman reined the pinto away from the stage, an arrow whistled through the air behind his head and clattered into the canyon wall to his right. He swung a look left as two painted braves clad in only loincloths, moccasins and war paint galloped their paint ponies through the notch in the canyon wall, screaming like devils loosed from hell. Their medicine pouches and bone necklaces jostled wildly.

As one jerked his mount to a skidding halt and reached into his quiver for another arrow, the other flung a war hatchet. Fargo reined the pinto toward the two braves as the hatchet careened wickedly past his left cheek to bury its head in the stage's thin housing.

The Trailsman snapped the Henry to his shoulder and fired two quick shots, firing and cocking and firing again. Hearing the braves scream but not waiting around to watch them fly off their horses, the Trailsman reined the Ovaro out ahead of the stage and gouged the stallion's flanks with his spurs.

"Keep your head down!" he ordered the girl as several arrows and bullets careened through the air around them, plunking into the dust on both sides of the two-track trail.

Fargo took his rifle in his right hand, reins in the left, then snaked that arm around the girl's waist, drawing her taut against him.

The Ovaro lowered its own head and, snorting, mane buffeting, lunged down the trail in a ground-eating gallop. This wasn't the stallion's first encounter with Indians, and the smell of blood and bear grease and the savage, elemental sound of the whoops and yowls and the creaking twang of bows and arrows chilled his blood and rendered his hooves light as feathers.

"What about the soldiers?" the girl cried above the thunder of the pinto's hooves.

"Finished!" Fargo shouted, turning in his saddle to fire his Henry repeater one-handed behind him, at the six or seven braves giving chase, hunkered low over the necks of their lunging ponies.

"What about my luggage?" she cried again. "All my belongings are on the *stage*!"

Two arrows thumped into the ground on both sides of the trail. Several slugs sliced the air over Fargo's head, one ricocheting loudly off a rock.

"If you want to go back for it, you're on your own!" Fargo shouted, loosing another shot behind.

"But . . . but . . . I have nothing to *wear*!"

Fargo jerked a look behind and shook the Ovaro's reins, urging more speed. "If we don't lose these savages, you won't *need* anything!"

As rifles popped behind him, he leaned forward to yell in the horse's ear. "Come on, boy! Split the trail *wide open*!"

The girl jerked her head toward the Trailsman accusingly, brows furrowed, lips parted, fire red hair jostling across her eyes. Fargo was about to ask what the look was about, but then he realized his left arm was pushing up beneath her naked breasts.

He gave a sheepish half smile, loosened his grip and turned to fling another shot behind them.

No other series packs this much heat!

THE TRAILSMAN

**Available wherever books are sold or at
penguin.com**